"Fear not: for I have redeemed thee, I have called thee by thy name; thou art mine.
When thou passest through the waters, I will be with thee; and through the rivers, they shall not overflow thee: when thou walkest through the fire, thou shalt not be burned; neither shall the flame kindle upon thee.
For I am the Lord thy God, the Holy One of Israel, thy Saviour."

—Isaiah 43:1–3 KJV

The Hidden Gate
A Fallen Petal

Savannah Secrets

A Fallen Petal

Ruth Logan Herne

Guideposts

Danbury, Connecticut

A Fallen Petal

Chapter One

"I CAN'T BELIEVE THE CEILING actually collapsed in my office," Julia Foley remarked as she typed furiously on the laptop she'd set up on the deck of Meredith Bellefontaine's historic Savannah home in early June. *Typed* may have been too generous a word for her actions.

Stabbed was more like it, and each finger poke made a tiny *click!* that punctuated Julia's frustration. She puffed out a breath against a wayward lock of pale silver hair and choked back a sigh. It came through, though, so she didn't choke it back all that well. "I appreciate that Arnold Mains is an old friend of yours, Mere, but that man does not understand how to move fast, and that's coming from a Southern woman. We are traditionally more understanding of such things but not at this moment."

"Bug infestation," Meredith lamented. "It seems the exterminator wasn't doing proper inspections or treatments for the past two years. He simply cashed my checks and gave a stamp of approval, so that brought the ceiling down."

"On my refurbished desk." Julia loved that desk. She'd brought it with her from Atlanta when she and her husband, Beau, decided the quieter setting of Savannah would suit them better. Despite its flaws, the old desk was perfect. An aged kneehole with a chestnut-toned finish and not one bit of gloss, exactly how she liked things.

I

Solid. Well made. Not showy. Now the poor thing was pockmarked with shots of wallboard all over the antique finish. But in the end, it was just a piece of furniture.

She shrugged. "It's fixable. And furniture is just furniture, after all. Still, the whole thing was a surprise and a disappointment. I was so excited to have my own office. My own desk again. In its own place, away from my house."

Meredith laughed. "I hear you, and it will happen soon. Just not as soon as we thought. Ron used to tell me I trust the wrong people, but then, he didn't trust too many, good or bad, so I suppose it evened out."

Meredith had lost her husband Ron almost two years ago. He'd died suddenly, leaving a gash in her heart and a thriving business that had ground to a standstill without him. A standstill, that is, until she and Julia decided to reopen and rename Ron Bellefontaine's private detective agency.

"Still, I should have double-checked the exterminator's reports. I didn't realize the company had changed hands right before Ron died."

"They should have sent a letter explaining that. That's the norm. This is on them, not you." Julia had spent years rendering decisions on guilt and innocence as a state-appointed juvenile court judge. She saw things in clear tones. Black-and-white worked for her, but occasionally she made way for life's grayer moments.

"They might have," Meredith replied. "I wasn't myself for a while, and there's probably a lot of stuff that got by me."

"Oh, honey, that's the way of it. And Ron was a law-and-order guy from the get-go, wasn't he?" Julia took a long draw on her Diet

Dr Pepper, then pressed the glass to her forehead. The coolness of the condensation felt good, but she was careful not to let it drip onto her keyboard.

"He was, and he hated red tape, which is why he left the police force and opened his own agency. Ron liked getting to the bottom of things, while I like trusting people—*most* people," she added firmly. "If we're running a business I have to make sure the i's are dotted and t's are crossed. Businesswomen can't afford costly mistakes."

"I just made sure it's costing us nothing but time," Julia crowed, then read aloud from her email. "'Dear Ms. Foley: While admitting no wrongdoing, Southeast Pest Control will cover the cost of all damage incurred at the aforementioned property and will refund the customer's retainers for the past two years. Per your request, payment for repairs will be made to Arnold Mains Construction.'"

"They caved?" Meredith's eyebrows shot up. An expression of relief eased the worry that had carved a W between her eyes since the weekend ceiling collapse. "So quickly? Do you think the title 'former Presiding Judge, Chatham County Juvenile Court' swayed them to make a swift decision?"

"Clout helps," Julia said cheerfully. "They probably figured I'm buddies with everyone in the county court system. Of course, that's nowhere near the truth, but if the implication pushed them to take responsibility, I'm fine with that. And they're lucky we don't sue them for time lost and potential loss of income, but that would be hard to prove since we just opened the business."

"Since we're only working from the house temporarily," added Meredith. "Let's just consider this a bump in the road for two entrepreneurs. No big deal."

"And we're in a gorgeous setting," Julia conceded, looking down at her keyboard. *Tap, tap, tap!* "Right here in the heart of Savannah's historic district with that pretty view of Troup Square. Who knows how many people will come seeking our help now that we've fixed things up so nicely with the Besset Plantation and sweet Maggie Lu?"

It felt wonderful to have their first case under their belt and a successful outcome. Meredith blotted her face with a folded square of paper towel. "May I ask again why we are conducting business on the deck when there is an expansive and delightfully air-conditioned living space just beyond that door?" She indicated the door of the house with a thrust of her chin. "June here in Georgia is not what some folks would consider porch friendly. Summer comes early. And stays a long while."

"We need to acclimate ourselves," Julia explained. "You and I are not the steel magnolias we used to be, and if we want to get Magnolia Investigations up and running, we've got to be prepared to 'glisten'"—she made air quotes with her fingers—"with the best of them. Lady detectives do not swoon, nor do they quietly retire to their fainting couches."

"And this is why we'll make a great team," Meredith declared. "You have all that big-city go-get-'em personality going on, and I like to delve into the nitty-gritty in the shadows. That's why this will work, Julia."

"That and the fact that you were a bigger part of some of Ron's cases than anyone knew," Julia said. She finished typing a reply to the exterminator and hit SEND. "Ron certainly showed a lot of wisdom and foresight when he made sure you got your certification years ago—"

4

"I suppose it was more to avoid a finger-pointing lawsuit than the thought that I was any kind of real help," Meredith cut in dryly.

Knowing Ron's Southern upbringing, Julia thought Meredith was probably right. Raised with fairly old-fashioned, traditional views regarding the roles of men, women, and genteel propriety, he loved his wife but turned a skeptical eye toward the importance of history. That was then, and Ron was more intrigued with the present. Julia nodded at Meredith. "I think he knew you'd help him any way you could but that you would be demure and stay behind the scenes. I know that's how you helped him with that case out near Fort Pulaski. Still, you and I both realize the days for demure are long gone."

"Drug smuggling under the guise of historic boat rides," declared Meredith. "That was simple from the get-go. Those captains didn't know Georgia history at all. That was a lucky find on my part."

"Not lucky. Smart," Julia corrected her. "Your work with the historical society gives you a deeper perspective on things, and if there's one thing I found out by being a judge, it's that many of today's misfortunes lie in the ruins of yesterday's crises. Some folks can muster up. Some can't. You have that cause-and-effect well in hand, Meredith, and that's not a gift. That's years of hard work and study bearing fruit."

Meredith smiled at her. "Well, thank you, my friend."

Despite growing up under Savannah's social norms, Meredith was quietly strong enough to be her own person most of the time, and her willingness to take this bold step forward should be wonderful for both of them.

"Ron was amazing with numbers," Julia noted as she finished clearing her inbox. "He came from money, he understood corporate financial structures, and he could smell an embezzling scheme like a hound on a raccoon. So his absence leaves us with a weak spot there," she added.

"Auditing and finance."

"Yes. Neither one of us has the nose or education for that kind of thing," Julia noted, "but if we get into a pinch, we've always got Wyatt." Wyatt was Julia's nephew, the son of her absentee sister. He'd become a CPA and accidentally fallen into the role of forensic auditing when he discovered a hidden deficit in a major corporation's finances. His discovery led the embezzlers to jail time and brought his firm multiple new clients and a sizable bonus for himself. "He's our backup quarterback, and speaking of football, are you keeping your season tickets for the Bulldogs?"

"You know, I think that was one of the biggest adjustments of widowhood," Meredith told her, but not with angst. Humor laced her tone more often now. "Getting used to fall weekends with no one yelling at the TV or rushing out the door on Saturday morning while lamenting game-day traffic. Have mercy, how that man loved his Bulldogs." She raised her glass but didn't sip it. Just held it. "I thought the boys would want to go, but they only managed one game last season. I'm not sure if that was lack of time or lack of interest, and I didn't have enough energy to second-market the seats. I'll see how this year goes. If Carter and Chase don't care to go, I'll drop the tickets. Some fan will be thrilled to get them."

Ron and Beau had gone to at least one game together each year. It had become a tradition. "I'm not pushing," Julia told her as she set the laptop aside. "Beau's friend Riley was asking. He noticed your seats were empty a lot last year. He's in the deck above you and would love to move down."

"Ron loved taking the boys when they were young. And he went through years of trading up to get better seats until he finally got the ones he wanted. It's funny how letting go of something I never used makes me feel like I'm closing the book on a whole chapter of life. Maybe that's why I was hoping the boys would use them, to keep some life in those ridiculously expensive seats." She rolled her eyes. "Of course, Carter and Chase are total opposites, so maybe they'd prefer alternate weeks. How can siblings be so completely different?"

Julia knew exactly how siblings could be that different. Her younger sister was nothing like her, and yet they shared two wonderful parents. "That's a question I've been asking for decades." Her dry tone highlighted her confusion. "And no pressure," Julia assured her. "You'll be able to sell them instantly, I'm sure. Just thought I'd mention there's a buyer waiting in the wings. Kind of like we'll be waiting on Arnold and his crew."

"There's no rushing the Mains."

"I see that," Julia muttered.

"Fortunately, entertaining clients in one's home is a perfectly acceptable practice. So we'll be relegated to the living room until the official office space is revamped."

"Of course you're right," Julia replied. "Blame my reluctance on my former career. Judges, prosecutors, and cops stay under the radar for a reason. We make people mad. Sometimes really mad. The Whitaker Street office gives us a measure of invisibility. In a business like this, a slight separation is never a bad idea." She tipped her black-rimmed glasses down and faced Meredith. "We're not exactly young, and it hasn't even been a year since your heart episode, my friend. I'm simply thinking an ounce of prevention isn't a bad idea. But you're right, it's only a few weeks' time, and I'm being a pest."

"The heart scare was my wake-up call, for certain," Meredith agreed. "It's what drove me to step aside from running the historical society after all those years. Did I want to help others, or preside over them? Old money talks here."

"Money talks anywhere, but old money whistles a sharp tune in the South," Julia noted. "Which might be another reason to keep the business away from your residence. Middle-aged women with money are easy targets."

"But we have our delightful Carmen with access to the internet and a fully stocked kitchen, and our gal does love to bake. This current situation could be in our favor."

Carmen Lopez was their Gal Friday for the office—once they had an office again—and that young Hispanic woman wasn't afraid to run a tight ship, speak her mind, or bake amazingly fun treats, three qualities her bosses liked and respected.

"You're right, of course." Julia sighed purposely this time. "I'm being silly by letting one minor setback bother me. We call it the 'courtroom curse.'" She aimed a wry look at Meredith. "When you're wearing a judicial robe, everyone listens. People jump. They snap to attention when you walk into a room. It's a head rush, and the reason we called it a curse is because you start expecting life to bend your way outside the courtroom. And life doesn't work that way. You're right—folks are just as likely to come knocking on a front door on East Charlton as they are to search out downtown. One thing I can say about our sweet city, it takes history seriously and makes it absolutely approachable."

"Except for the inevitable family scandals and closet skeletons," Meredith noted. "Every old Southern family has some, and most are adept at hiding them."

"Until the past comes creeping up on the present." Julia paused and looked down from the raised deck overlooking the historic park-like square. "Speaking of the past, isn't that Harlowe Green coming our way?"

"Oh my word, it is."

Julia followed close on Meredith's heels as Meredith hurried down the steps to meet the elderly gentleman. Harlowe had the somewhat dubious honor of being the oldest person in Savannah, and at one hundred and four years old, he was an amazing figure as he clomped around town with his walker. He'd hired a young man to drive him places, and a housekeeper, who also played the keyboard at Julia's church, tended his Historic District home. However, Harlowe prided himself on doing as much as he could himself. Meredith's deck steps, however, would have bested the aged fellow.

Meredith reached him on one side, as Julia took the other. "Harlowe, good morning." Meredith took the aged gentleman's right arm gently. "Were you coming to call on me?"

He gazed at her.

Then Julia.

Then Meredith again. And then he did something that grabbed Julia's heart.

He started crying.

Chapter Two

Tears welled up in honey-brown eyes set beneath thickly arched snow-white eyebrows. A thatch of white hair rimmed Harlowe's bald head, a wild look that seemed to suit the old fellow, and while Julia wasn't easily swayed to sympathy, the sight of the old-timer's tears tugged her that way.

"Are you ill, my friend? Do you need a doctor? An ambulance? What hurts, Harlowe?" Meredith kept her voice soft and soothing. She'd always been better at that than Julia.

"Here." The old man put his right hand over his heart. "It hurts here."

"Heart attack," Meredith declared. "Julia, I left my phone in the house. You stay with Harlowe, I'll call 911."

"You have to start remembering to grab your phone, Mere. No worries, I've got mine," Julia told her.

It took a few seconds to wrestle her phone out of her pocket, just long enough for Harlowe to scowl and almost bellow, "I'm not havin' a heart attack, young lady. If I was succumbing to that particular ailment, would I be chasing up the road with my walker to tell you about it?"

The old goat was yelling at her.

Although he *did* call her a young lady, so she didn't deck him on the spot, and Julia gave herself extra points for that.

Nobody yelled at her and got away with it. She narrowed her gaze, stared him down, and replied in her best courtroom voice. "I expect you wouldn't have, although you clearly clapped a hand to your heart, and you're about the oldest thing I've seen other than a few local buildings, so how is one to know what you mean, kind sir?"

"Up there." He pointed to the deck as if it offered respite. "Let's talk up there. Or inside. And you could have thought to put a ramp along the side here, if you're set on hanging out a shingle, Meredith."

"You know we're reopening the agency?" Meredith asked as she extended her arm toward him. "Grab on, Harlowe. Let's talk."

"And mine too," said Julia as she copied Meredith's gesture.

The old man gave Julia an affronted look but accepted her offer. Together, they got him up the steps with only a small measure of difficulty on the very top one, when the doddering fellow almost tumbled backward. He would have taken the two women with him too, except Meredith had the good sense to grab hold of the deck rail as she took that last step. Her grip kept them upright when gravity had other ideas.

Once they'd regained their balance, Julia guided Harlowe to the wide-backed wicker chair she'd been using. Meredith took her seat, and Julia perched a hip on the rail after retrieving Harlowe's walker and placing it near his chair. "Now what's going on, my friend?" asked Meredith. "No one can hear you up here."

Harlowe faced Meredith. Tears welled in his eyes again. Julia hurried inside to the kitchen, then back out with a box of soft tissues. "They're kind to your nose," she assured him as she set the box on the patio-style table between the chairs.

"At my age, kindness of any sort is a blessing." He sent her a watery smile, used several tissues, then sighed. "I need your help."

"Ours to give, if we can," Meredith assured him.

Julia nodded but stayed quiet.

"My great-grandniece told me you're thinking of getting Ron's old business up and running again, and while Ron was a good man, I knew you were the one with a gift for some things," he told Meredith frankly. "If it came to dusty corners or hidden alcoves, it was you who found a way to unearth the secrets of the past."

"We were just discussing that," Meredith replied. "The South likes to keep some secrets hidden, while flaunting others. We are our own conundrum at times. What's this all about?"

"Someone's been doing some digging," he told them. "Coming around, asking questions, fishing for answers, and he won't let up. Says his name is Jem Baldwin, and he wants to write a book about me. Us. The Greens."

"Jem Baldwin, the *New York Times* best-selling author of *Sleep Well, Sweet South*?" Julia stared at him, eyes wide. "He wants to base one of his bestselling novels on you? And your family? Why aren't you singing a hallelujah chorus, Mr. Green? He's world renowned."

"In a time when everyone knows everything about you, there are some things that might be best left uncovered," he whispered. "But his probing means the not knowing will come to an end, and that's why I'm here." He fished in the walker's cleverly attached pocket and pulled out an old slate-gray cardboard sleeve. With frail, trembling fingers he withdrew a faded black-and-white image. He held it out for both of them to see.

It was a photograph of a grinning little boy. Wide-eyed, he seemed to pose reluctantly, as if there was so much more to see and do. The photographer managed to catch his essence, as if captured midmoment, pausing only long enough to appease a parent or whoever commissioned the picture. It wasn't hard to imagine a precocious side to this child, and Meredith smiled in recognition. "He's an engaging little thing, isn't he?" She passed the picture to Julia, and Julia agreed instantly.

"Oh, that look!" She smiled. "As if he's grudgingly giving the photographer enough time to snap the photo and then get out of his way because he's got things to do. Who is he?"

"My brother."

Meredith frowned. "I didn't know you had a brother, Harlowe. I've never heard mention of him. I only knew about Bertha and Wilma, your younger sisters."

"No one's heard mention of him, because no one knows."

The way he said the words—or maybe the expression of complete loss as he said the words—sent a shiver down Julia's spine.

"He disappeared when I was five. I barely remembered him myself, you see, and when I'd ask about him, I'd be shushed. As if I wasn't supposed to ask. He disappeared, and all of his stuff went too. It was like he vanished. When I got a little older and asked about him, my parents would look surprised and say 'you must be thinking of your cousin LeRoy, Harlowe. He used to come by and play with you a lot.'" He gripped the tissues tightly in his hand. "I knew I wasn't thinking of LeRoy. I was thinking of Lawrence and how we climbed railings, and we pretended we were shipwrecked and sharks were trying to eat us and we had to get from the old carriage house to the house without touching the ground, and that meant shimmying fence posts and shuffling along fence boards, then jumping from thing to thing to avoid the grass."

"My boys played a similar game." Meredith laid a hand on his arm. "How are you so sure that it was Lawrence and not LeRoy, Harlowe? The names are somewhat similar."

"At first I was sure because it was my brother." His plain talk spoke to the common sense of that assertion. "Then, when I got a little older, I wasn't sure, because why would people keep telling me it wasn't him? So I dropped it, but one day, when LeRoy and I were working on a project for his house, I asked him about that game." He was staring down at the wadded tissues, then brought his attention back to Meredith. "He had no idea what I was talking about. He stared at me, blank-like, and I knew right then that LeRoy and I had never played that game. That Lawrence existed somewhere. Wilma was a toddler when he and I played together, so she had no memory of him at all, and Bertha wasn't born yet, but I was the oldest, and Lawrence and I were best friends. I loved my sisters, don't get me wrong, but a brother—" He wiped his eyes. "When he disappeared, no one ever spoke of him again. There were no pictures. No remembrances on his birthday. Nor would they even allow me the memory of him. But what kind of person would do that? Wipe a child off the face of the earth like that?"

"You've looked for him before?" Julia asked.

"I looked here and there when I was a younger man, but I couldn't find any records through the normal channels. In the South, if there's a secret to be kept, it's kept."

No question about that. And it was very hard to uncover records before the world of internet technology opened up DNA and heritage sites that linked people.

"A part of me didn't want to make waves for my parents. How was I to know what I'd find?" He lifted his thin shoulders in a shrug.

"Longevity being what it is in our family, by the time my parents passed on, I was too old to do a lot of exploring. But it's haunted me every day, and now I've got this writer fellow buzzing around, dragging things up." That thought deepened the wrinkle between his eyes noticeably. "With my days drawing short, I need to find out what happened to my brother."

He turned so he could face both women. "I don't know if he was killed. Or if there was an accident, and maybe Mother couldn't bear to talk about it because of the pain. And that's another problem. Back then, folks didn't talk about things, everything was hushed up. I did the simple things about twenty-five years ago. I hunted for a birth record and searched for anything that might turn him up, and I found nothing, but now is different." He indicated the phone in Julia's hand. "Everything is traceable now."

Julia grimaced. "There are still some untraceable things out there. And we're talking nearly a hundred years ago, correct?"

"I was born in 1916, and Lawrence the year after. There wasn't much time between us," he noted, but then he turned a more animated expression toward Meredith. "That's where you come in. I always knew that when it came to old stuff, it wasn't Ron Bellefontaine combing through annals and dusty old books. Just like it wasn't him tending those pretty window boxes of yours that do this square proud."

The mention of her sumptuous window gardens inspired Meredith's smile. "I don't mind getting my hands dirty, and gardening is great therapy. City plots are self-limiting by their size, and tending those window boxes makes me happy."

"When I heard you two ladies were going to resurrect the agency, I knew I had to come to you. Find him. Please." He wasn't afraid to beg, and his entreaty seemed to grab Meredith's heart. That was all right, because Julia's emotions were drawn too. "It's not that I don't have money to pay a different agency. You know I do."

Meredith acknowledged that with a dip of her chin and looked at Julia. Julia knew what she was thinking. Another missing child? So soon after Harriet? What were the odds of that happening?

"It's that finding a lost child is more delicate than one would ever expect, and if anyone ever finds him, I want it to be you. Both of you," he added, including Julia in his look. "The two of you searching for a lost little boy is about the best way I can imagine of finding him. Finding my brother."

Meredith broached the next topic gently. "It's a very old case, Harlowe. I want you to understand that—"

He didn't let her finish. "He's gone. Gone home to the Lord, I expect, and I've known that to be likely, but I think God kept me here, healthy enough to see you two take up business once this fellow started snooping around. I think He let me live long enough to find Lawrence before He calls me home. And as long as I've got breath left to breathe, I intend to do it. If you ladies will help me, that is."

Julia inhaled, long and slow.

Then she met Meredith's gaze across the shaded deck. She didn't say a word, but she blinked once. That blink said enough. Meredith redirected her attention back to her bighearted neighbor. "We'll do it, Harlowe."

Oh, that old man's face when she said those words. As if they'd just given him a reprieve.

"I don't know that we'll be successful," Meredith went on. "Old records have a way of getting lost or destroyed. The South is famous for its fires and hurricanes, tornadoes and flooding. But your family hasn't moved around a lot, and there are several people from your nieces' and nephews' generation still alive, so we'll see what we can find. If Lawrence was with your family until this age..." She raised the picture of the preschooler. "Someone remembers something, and Julia and I have been on the planet long enough to know one thing. Two folks can keep a secret..."

"If one of them is dead," Julia finished. "People love to talk, even if it's to assuage their conscience. Someone, somewhere, knows what happened to this child, and we'll do everything we can to find the truth. So help me, God."

Those words took her straight back into her courtroom, but she meant them sincerely. To solve this puzzle they'd need all the help they could get. Once they'd helped Harlowe down the front steps and walked him home to his house down the street, they came back to the deck.

Julia said nothing about needing an office.

Neither did Meredith.

They got up the steps, and Julia raised a hand for a high five. "Girlfriend," she said, letting a little Southern flair elongate the word.

Meredith slapped hands with her and drawled, "We have gone and got ourselves another case!"

"And what a case it is." Julia studied the photo Harlowe had left with them. "Do we even have a chance of solving it?"

Meredith studied the picture too. "Jules." She used the old nickname easily. "We might, at that. There's something familiar about this picture, the cardboard sleeve it's in. Like I've seen this exact sleeve before, with a photographer's notation at the lower right corner."

"From a case with Ron? Or the historical society, maybe?"

Meredith frowned. "I don't know, but the clarity of this picture means it's been preserved intentionally. Who did that? And why? Would a child have the presence of mind to safely hide a picture for three generations?" she wondered. "And if not, how did Harlowe find it?"

A great question. One they would have to ask Harlowe at their next meeting.

"Grab your keys, Julia. I say we get copies of this photograph made right away, just in case."

"Agreed. And then study them with a celebratory high-end coffee under a shady tree," said Julia.

"All good, except the shady tree part," Meredith said cheerfully. She called inside to get Carmen's coffee order, then came back outside. "We'll have our coffee on the run since Harlowe Green is on borrowed time. Let's just say he's not of an age to buy green bananas, so we don't dare waste a moment."

Julia saw the sense in that and grinned. "Point taken. I'll drive, and you tell me everything you know about the Greens on the way. And then we begin."

April 1921

Dearest Virginia,

My suspicions increase of late.

What began as a normal and wonderful position with a highly regarded family has become difficult and confusing. Maybe three children in quick succession is too much for

Patrice, and yet she seemed fine until this past winter. Her mother gone home to the Lord and now a new baby on the way.

Is that it? Too much stress on a kindhearted young woman? I cannot say, but she is not herself. Worry creases her brow, and she's grown sharp with the children. Lawrence tests his boundaries daily or more. He's a handful, that one. His father calls him bright. He is that, but obstinate too, and in need of a firm hand. And Wilma bears watching all the time. She's an inquisitive little girl. Keeping her out of harm's way is a job in itself.

Is it the loss of her mother that makes sadness dog Patrice's days? It is a sorrowful thing to lose one's mother, for the good Lord grants us but one, and with Mr. Sully gone to Charleston so often, the sorrow seems to deepen its grip. I've been slipping treats to Master Lawrence on the sly. It is my contention that showing the boy kindness and love should be the expectation. Not the exception. But I am suddenly alone in this endeavor, and I can't think why.

It will pass, I'm sure. Once the baby is safely here, we'll work hand in hand again, for Patrice Green is far more than my employer. She has become a trusted friend.

I pray all is well with you, my beloved sister, and would wish the distance away if I could, but I cannot, so letters must suffice.

Your darling younger sister,
Carolina

Chapter Three

THE SCENT OF FRESHLY BAKED chocolate chip cookies was enough to keep Carmen on the payroll forever, Julia decided as she and Meredith returned to the house for a strategy session. The young woman's frank demeanor, honesty, baking, and humor made a complete package.

"A one-hundred-year-old case?" Carmen was never one to hold back, and the look she gave Julia and Meredith spoke volumes. "There aren't enough modern-day bad guys for you ladies to hunt down? Because I've lived the downside of life for half the time I've been on the planet, and I'm here to tell you there are."

"History is Meredith's particular specialty," teased Julia. "But a centennial mystery might put her to the test. And this crusty old fellow thumped right over here with his walker, making it hard to say no. But where do we begin? And if you say the library, I may throw something at you," she noted as Meredith tapped something into her phone.

"First we procure two DNA samples from Harlowe to send to the ancestry registries. We can buy one of the kits locally, but the other one is online sales only, so I just ordered it with expedited shipping. Should be here tomorrow." Meredith held up her phone to indicate her completed purchase.

"Brilliant."

"Why, thank you." Meredith preened. "Then the library and the newspaper archives, the museum, and anything that may have been entered online concerning Savannah history and the Greens and the child in particular."

"Kids don't just disappear." Carmen set a tray of warm cookies on the counter. "And you said there were three other children?"

"Yes. Harlowe and his two little sisters." Meredith set her mug of coffee on the kitchen island and reached for a cookie.

"There are cooling ones on the table. Those will burn your fingers," Carmen advised. "You two talk. I'll go pretend I'm busy in the next room and can't hear you."

"As long as you take a vow of silence—"

"Like being in a convent."

Julia laughed. "Why do I not see that as your destiny, Carmen?" The two exchanged grins. Julia had taken Carmen under her wing years before. She'd been orphaned at age ten and wasn't a fan of the foster care system. She'd gone her own way multiple times and finally ended up in Julia's courtroom as a miscreant. Now she was a sharp, funny, educated young woman with a discerning mind and a keen faith. It had all worked out quite well in the end.

"Of course you can stay here and listen," Meredith told her around a bite of cookie. "You're going to be working on research and finding things, so you can't exactly be out of the loop unless it's something dangerous."

Carmen struck a pose. "Danger is my middle name."

"It was," noted Julia. "And then you chose to walk the straight and narrow. Well done, by the way."

Carmen beamed. "Thank you. I do like being on this side of the law. So if you're looking for information, I can do internet legwork for you and send you pertinent links. Screening might save you time, and we all know that time is money."

"Got that right." Julia sipped her iced coffee, thoughtful. "Let's put visiting the house they lived in on the top of the list. A visual of the setting always helps me see cases better."

"Except they don't own it anymore," Meredith said. "So that's a dead end."

"Not if you explain the situation and they let you in," suggested Carmen.

"Like just show up at their door?"

"Um. Yes. That's my suggestion." Carmen didn't try to hide the disbelief in her voice. "You're really giving up that easily?"

"Not giving up, exactly," Meredith began, but Julia interrupted.

"She's right, we need to get into that house, but how? Breaking and entering seems extreme."

Carmen's gaze flicked from one to the other, then back again. "Neither one of you has ever worked as a domestic, I take it?"

"I was a paper shuffler in college. Then I got started at the museum and helped Ron and raised the boys, but I always had household help. I never worked as household help," Meredith admitted.

"And you worked for me, so you know I've never done domestic work," noted Julia. "So—"

"Are you thinking what I'm thinking?" asked Meredith, looking at Julia.

"I am," Julia answered. "We have Carmen apply for a position at the Greens' old house."

"What?" Carmen slid another tray of cookies into the oven and set the timer. "How about 'no'?"

"Your cookies alone could win you a position."

"Except they're probably not looking for help. This is so random. What are you two thinking?"

"You said you want to help when you can," Meredith reminded her.

"And everyone's looking for help these days, because no one shows up for work anymore," Julia asserted. "Odds are that someone in that big house is in need of something."

"So I show up at their door, unsought and uninvited." Carmen's dour expression made her feelings clear on that.

"All right, let's leave that for the moment," Meredith declared. "I say head right over to the library and then the newspaper, then we'll stop by Target and buy an ancestry kit. We'll have Harlowe give samples tomorrow when we have both kits. Is Beau golfing today?"

"Fishing. Gone for three days."

"So supper at the diner?" suggested Meredith. "Early-bird special?"

Carmen muttered something under her breath, but Julia just laughed.

"Guard the pennies, and the dollars will come," Meredith told Carmen. "And dinner's on me, so you don't have to worry about paying. One of the perks."

"I'm on board with that, except I've got a date tonight."

"A date?" Meredith sat right down and leaned in.

Julia did the exact same thing. "With who?"

Carmen slid the last tray of cookies onto a hot pad then set her elbows on the counter and faced them. "Harmony." When they stared at her, she relaxed into a smile. "She's a little girl in foster care. Six years old. Her mama's in prison and daddy is gone. I've signed on to be her mentor with the Boys & Girls Club, so I'll get to take her places. Do things with her. Maybe help her to feel special about who she is."

"Oh, Carmen, what a wonderful way to give back," exclaimed Julia. "That's perfect, sweetie."

"Well, I'm new at this, but my experience in foster care taught me there's no such thing as too much love. And now I'm gainfully employed, I've got a car, and there are so many places to see around here. Even little things like letting her help me bake."

"Those simple things are sometimes best, aren't they?"

Carmen didn't get teary-eyed. She rarely did. But she looked sentimental as she agreed. "I would have given anything to have one more day of baking with Mami. So now I can bake for others, and Harmony can help."

"I love it," Julia declared. "The whole thing makes me smile, Carmen. And if you find she's in need of anything, I'd love to play fairy godmother."

"Me too!" Meredith beamed at the thought, then stood. "All right, let's head out from here. Carmen, we'd love to have you bring Harmony to the diner for supper. She might get a kick out of that."

Carmen didn't refuse, but the unconvinced lift of her brows sent the message. "Yup, a busy six-year-old in a diner with hundred-year-old mystery talk buzzing around. I can see how that would be awesome for her."

"Point taken. See you tomorrow, and thank you for baking."

"Well, once the phone is ringing off the hook, this might not happen all that often, but for the moment, there's time to do it and tuck them into the freezer. Then we have a stockpile when it's too busy to bake. And I expect that will be soon."

Would it?

Julia wasn't sure, but she hadn't felt this invigorated since her last day in the courtroom. And that in itself felt marvelous.

Chapter Four

"YOU TWO LOOK FAR TOO eager to be here for this to be a social visit," Rebecca Thompson drawled when she spotted Julia and Meredith moving toward her. The women had met Rebecca the month before, while working their first case, and they'd sparked an almost instant friendship with her and Maggie Lu King, an amazing library volunteer. "Julia, you've got a big-city style about you that fits wherever you go. Where on earth did you get that scarf? It shrieks style. Please tell me it's a knockoff and therefore affordable."

Julia grimaced. "Not a knockoff but a gift from Beau, so I never saw the price tag. The guy loves me, but he probably had one of the nurses find it on the internet."

"The only thing my husband searches for on the web are replacement parts," Rebecca lamented. "Parts for the mower, for the Weedwacker, for the furnace. Fortunately he's bested by the AC, so that gets the professional help it deserves when one of the units goes down. So what are you two looking for? And if you extend a dinner invite to me, I'll jump on board. Kelvin is working tonight."

Rebecca's husband Kelvin was known as "The Voice of the Savannah." He narrated scenic dinner cruises as they rolled up and down the Savannah River. Kelvin's love of history and distinct persona made him a local icon. He wasn't a young man by any means.

He was a dozen years older than his wife, and Rebecca was sixty-four, but there was something about Kelvin's mustachioed look, gray hair, and his love and knowledge of history that made him perfect in his narrative role. "I reminded him to take plenty of bug spray. Not for the ship, of course, but the walk back to his car."

"We're having supper at the diner."

"And I can already taste Charlene's chicken and dumplings, a favorite that will keep me from ever being a thin woman," Rebecca noted as Boog Simpson approached the desk.

"It's too sultry for such weighty blends," he explained in one of those butt-in voices that tried to take charge even when things were none of his business. "That is a September dish, and I've said that to Charlene often enough, but it seems folks will order as they choose, regardless. And I suppose the season isn't the big deal it used to be," he continued, "although a mixed-greens salad dressed with grilled chicken and vinaigrette is always a summertime preference."

"Air-conditioning." Rebecca appeased the former food editor for the *Tribune* with a look of understanding. "When it's cool as a cucumber inside, everything tastes good, doesn't it? That way people don't feel as constrained about what they order."

"Doesn't make it right." He dipped his chin in a faint act of politeness. "Ladies." He moved on and out the door.

Julia didn't dare look at Meredith or Rebecca.

This was a library, after all, and the rules for quiet were still in existence out here in the main area, but when they got to the new addition, she started giggling. "I can't..." She waved a hand, bent over, laughed, then stood up again. "Oh my word, I'm sorry, but when did critiquing food become such a pompous state of affairs?" she asked.

Rebecca hooked a thumb toward the bank of computers behind them. "It's more about when it stopped," she told Julia. "Food critics were the big thing for a long time, and restaurant critics in the South were highly regarded before everyone was sharing their opinions online. Now no one cares what one purported food expert says about a dive, a diner, or a five-star establishment, since we can all hop online and check out a hundred Google reviews. He was asked to retire early, and I heard he was working at one of the hotels, trying to upgrade the way they treated their guests and redevelop their restaurants."

"I didn't know he lost his job. Now I feel dreadful for laughing," Julia told them.

"Changing times. Rules slip out the door as technology flies in the window," said Meredith. "So, Becca. Where can we find out the best and fastest information possible about the Green family? Sully and Patrice and the kids."

"There's a lot on both of them," Rebecca replied. She led them to the computer area. "Sully was a big contributor to all kinds of things, although Carnegie was the major source of funds for this particular library," she told them. "Still, Sully Green left his mark as a philanthropist, a financier, a real estate investor, and a lover of the arts. Theater, music, live shows. He and Patrice frequented a lot of performances over the years and sponsored many of them to come here."

"He loved his wife."

"A fairy-tale romance," Rebecca declared. "He tried to never go away without taking her unless it was just plain too far, and he always hurried back. And they were most often seen together, a beautiful partnership. She died first, you know."

Julia shook her head. "I didn't know that."

"She went downhill in the early nineties, and Sully stayed right by her side the whole while. He died a few years later, just shy of his one hundredth birthday. It's funny that you're asking about them, because you will never guess who else was in here asking questions about the Greens."

"Jem Baldwin?"

Rebecca's mouth dropped open, and she narrowed her eyes. "You know he's in town?"

"Let's just say we know he's researching the Green family too. We don't want to get in his way," began Julia.

"But we also don't want him in ours," finished Meredith. "Newcomers, butting into all our ways and means and history as if it belonged to them. Preposterous."

Rebecca lifted an eyebrow. "You're searching for something, aren't you? Something to do with the Greens."

Her question caught Julia by surprise. Of course Rebecca would figure out they were on the hunt for something, but Harlowe had been adamant about keeping things low key. Problem was, once you started digging in Georgian soil, ubiquitous red clay muddied what could have been clean water.

"We're more like clearing a path," Meredith assured her, and the tightness in Julia's gut eased. "If Jem Baldwin is writing a book about Harlowe's family, our old friend just wants to get ahead of the game and make sure that respect is given where it's due."

"As it should be," Rebecca agreed. "And in a moment of rare professionalism, I made sure he knew that. I didn't want him to be put off about researching here. But we know"—Rebecca drew out the word as she moved toward the computers—"that when we're talking a century back, there were secrets, my friends. Many things have changed for the better, including this sweet library. When the big library was built in 1904, blacks weren't allowed inside, and nearly fifty percent of Savannah's population were people of color. The disparity was not lost on the very vibrant African American population, and they lobbied for their own library. It finally opened ten years later, with fundraising help from the black community and Mr. Carnegie himself. Later, folks like the Greens offered donations as well, but even though these old halls were given financial support from the city, they had a separate board to oversee this location, because its designation was as a 'Coloreds' library."

"And now it's open for all, as are all the branches in the Live Oak Library system," noted Julia. "So, Rebecca, since you're not under a vow of silence or anything, what was Jem Baldwin researching?"

"Well, the Greens, of course, but you already know that."

"What aspects?" Meredith asked. "Do you think he's staying close by? All the Live Oak libraries can access the local historical database, so why is he doing his research here? A best-selling author hanging out on lower East Henry?" She shook her head. "This isn't exactly the Upper East Side," she went on, referring to the upscale Manhattan community Jem Baldwin called home.

"Proximity would be my guess," said Rebecca. "When he was pulling out his phone, he dropped a parking stub from the lot that

Eliza Stevens uses for her B and B guests. My guess is he's staying close to his research."

"Makes sense," added Julia. She indicated the small bank of computers with a dip of her chin. "I don't suppose you can show us which computer he was using?"

"Don't you think he'd wipe his search history?" Meredith asked, but she moved toward the closest carrel. A look from Rebecca made her shift two computers to the right, and when she sat down and woke up the monitor, she gasped in surprise. She was looking at a local history website showing results for a search of SULLIVAN GREEN. "He never logged off." She brought up the browser history. "And this is all basic family history, but he's even gone to the ancestry sites." She turned and raised both brows at Julia and Rebecca. "And there's a lot of info here."

"Well, if he's doing a family saga loosely based on the Greens, then that makes sense," noted Rebecca. "Remember James Michener's sagas?"

"I still have my original copy of *Hawaii*," Julia replied. "The way he delved into history and setting made me realize I was better off being an avid reader than writing the great American novel. I didn't have time or patience to put in that much work."

"Exactly, but look how much easier that research is now, with the internet and genealogy databases. A few clicks and less than a hundred dollars—"

"Paid for by his publisher, no doubt."

"And you're totally enmeshed with time, places, dates, relatives. A whole family tree at your fingertips, right back to the original Irish ancestors."

"Julia, how about if you use that computer." Meredith pointed to the desktop to her left.

"Because you hate having someone looking over your shoulder," Julia said, and Meredith nodded.

"I surely do, and if I send you the links to half the pages, we can double-team this and come up with maybe an idea about where he's going with all of this."

Julia took a seat at the adjacent computer. Rebecca started back for the main area. "I'll leave you to it, and I'll see you at the diner later. What time?"

"Five fifteen."

"Perfect. I'm off at four thirty, so that gives me time to stop by the pharmacy for Kelvin's prescription and pick up some greeting cards. Two upcoming weddings, two summer birthdays, and—" She paused, suddenly awkward, and Meredith looked up. She must have read Rebecca's expression, because she filled in the blank.

"Sympathy cards."

Rebecca frowned, chagrined.

"It's all right," Meredith assured her. "I have a stash at home too. If there is one sure thing about this life, it's that nothing is sure except the good Lord's love for us. You get your cards, and we'll all hope you don't have to use them anytime soon."

"See you later."

"Yes."

Julia scanned page after page on her monitor and came up with nothing. The ancestry pages yielded great facts about the Green family but nothing about a baby boy born in 1917. And when she went to some of the more obscure sites that Jem Baldwin had gone to, it was primarily a mishmash of social functions that Sully and Patrice attended.

She was about to call this a fruitless effort when one photograph stood out.

She pulled up a page featuring Sully and Patrice at a ceremony for what used to be the Georgia Infirmary, the first hospital ever erected for people of color. Men in suits dominated the photograph. The caption below listed the community leaders pictured and several major contributors, including Sully and Patrice.

It was wonderful to see a photograph of blacks and whites working together for a common goal, but that wasn't what drew Julia's attention. It was the grief on Patrice Green's pretty face as the plaque marking the one hundredth anniversary of the Georgia Infirmary was set into place.

With a few clicks she sent the picture to the printer, and when she had the enlarged copy in her hands, she studied it closely.

Sully was focused on the ceremony, but he had a loving arm around his wife's slim shoulders.

Everyone else was smiling proudly for the camera, taking their moment of fame.

Not Patrice.

She looked downhearted. Almost devastated.

"Let's be sure to clear our history before we go," Meredith said. Both women did so and logged off, then Meredith leaned around and peered at the picture in Julia's hand. "What did you print?"

Julia handed it over without a word. Would Meredith notice what she'd zeroed in on? Or had the camera simply freeze-framed Patrice between looks, and the photographer went with it?

Meredith immediately pointed to Patrice. "She looks so distraught, doesn't she?"

"I saw that too."

Meredith scanned the date. "Harlowe would be about sixteen years old when this was taken."

"Is that significant?" Julia whispered.

Meredith made a face. "I don't know. If his brother died in 1921 or so, that's an eleven-year span. Unless another tragedy befell the family?"

"Or her expression could be coincidental and have nothing to do with what we're looking for."

"And yet it's so sad," Meredith whispered. "Heartbreakingly sad."

"Exactly why I printed it. Meredith…" A sudden chill from the AC had Julia folding her arms across her chest. But maybe it wasn't from the air-conditioning vent above them. Maybe it was the thought she was about to express. "You don't suppose they might have institutionalized that little boy, do you? I hate to even say such a thing, but it wasn't an uncommon practice back then. If a child had a condition the family couldn't deal with, they put them into a home or rest care facility."

"And at the height of the eugenics movement too."

The eugenics movement had taken root in the United States and other countries, looking to cleanse the genetic pool by separating or sterilizing anyone deemed "feebleminded." It was a horrific stain on history that fed into Hitler's rhetoric and case for a supreme Aryan race.

A deep frown formed a firm W between Meredith's eyes. "Julia, I hadn't considered that, but you're right. The time frame fits. It was considered unseemly for a family to produce an imperfect child."

"Would Harlowe have realized there was something wrong if that was the case?"

34

"Possibly not, but even if he had, ninety-nine years might have wiped that slate clean." She jotted down a couple of things in her notebook. "I don't see anything in Jem's browsing history that suggests he was looking for something like that."

"Which could mean he doesn't know about Lawrence."

"If he existed. Maybe we'd be wise to take that with a slight grain of salt ourselves. And yet Harlowe seems quite sure."

"Having a beloved person disappear is traumatic enough to create a firm memory, even at that age," Julia said softly. "I saw a lot of that in the courtroom, and science bears it out. Memories associated with negative outcomes or trauma generally seat themselves firmly, even if we try to block them."

"You know these days it's hard for anyone to vanish. With technology being what it is, most folks leave some kind of digital or real footprint, but back then it wasn't all that uncommon, unfortunately." Meredith glanced at her watch. "It's almost closing time. Let's pay for that print," she said as Julia slipped the print into a plain manila folder. "And head over to the diner to get a table, okay?"

"Yes." Julia turned to cross the library as Jem Baldwin strode through the front doors, looking every bit the famous author he was, and he wasn't headed toward Rebecca and the other clerk at the front desk.

No.

He was headed right for them and probably about to discover they knew what he'd been researching. But who knew he was coming back?

Julia grabbed Meredith's hand, hurried her through the smaller access door labeled EMPLOYEES ONLY, and out the back door.

Savannah, Georgia
September 1921

Darkness bathed Savannah's thick-shaded streets as Carolina Lambert slipped from tree to tree. Her banged-up old suitcase listed her to the right, but that wasn't the bag of concern.

It was the smaller one, slung beneath a cape she didn't need in the warmth of a Georgia September, but with her job gone, her single bag packed, and little hope for a new placement in a town the Greens practically ruled, she had no choice but to don the wrap, sure to need it sometime.

She wanted to hurry to the depot and put as much space between her and Patrice Green as possible. Patrice, her friend and employer, now her worst enemy? Unbelievable.

"Need a ride, miss?" a cabby called from the other side of the road. His horse stomped a foot, eager to move, but the unexpected voice set her heart racing. She shook her head and kept moving, trying to hurry.

She couldn't. The weighty bag and her tired soul held her back, and she didn't dare waste money to hire a ride. Money would be scarce now, at least for a while. And maybe forever. A woman in her late twenties with no credentials wouldn't find work easily. Not in the South, where those recommendations meant so very much. Genteel Southern families were quite particular about references. She didn't know if it would be the same in the north. She hoped not, but there could be no staying here. Not with what she knew.

She clutched the small bag more tightly to her chest and pushed along the least-lit streets, in case someone figured out what she had done. Sully and Patrice had let her go purposely. That was no secret.

The secret lay tucked against her chest, beneath the very arm that used to cradle her dear friend's babies. First Harlowe. Then Lawrence. Then funny little Wilma, with her heart-winning smile.

But it all changed after the northern vacation. Everything changed. Not just the number of family members, but Patrice. Sully. And a sorrowful and sad little boy who walked around as if his little heart had just been broken, and a child no one spoke of. A child gone. His history wiped out.

Carolina had stayed in Savannah with Wilma. Harlowe was supposed to stay too, but at the last minute Sully gave in and let him go far enough with them and Lawrence to visit his northern grandparents.

And when they came back, only Harlowe came with them.

Patrice retired to her room, sorrowful and mute.

Hushed voices spoke of tragedy, but the staff was given warnings not to ask questions, and of course they didn't, because everyone on their small staff loved Patrice and Sully.

But where was that precious, precocious child? If something happened to him, why didn't they bring him back to the beautiful monument area in Stafford Park where generations of Greens lay buried?

Patrice, sick with pregnancy, sick with life, still sorrowing the loss of her mother six months before, lay overwhelmed in bed, staring at nothing.

Sully, such a good man, distraught and worried and desperately trying to keep things together.

Harlowe, too young to realize he shouldn't ask questions, asked away. They lied to him. Outright, really, after shushing him nonstop, and that was when she went to Patrice, her friend and employer, and begged for the truth just so the firstborn would be able to move on with life.

Sacked.

Within hours.

Not because of what she'd carefully retrieved from the burn barrel the gardener had been instructed to use the week before, but because she dared question Patrice.

So here she was, with little money, a few clothes, and a secret. A secret so wretched she couldn't bear to keep it, but keep it she must, as the hands of Southern nobility and wealth could still reach the north. But it was a big country, and growing daily. If she hid herself quietly and maintained her silence, she'd be all right. She'd have to be. Right now, that was her only hope.

Chapter Five

"WE DIDN'T PAY FOR THE COPY," Meredith protested as Julia hustled toward her car.

"I'll give Becca the money at the diner," Julia replied as Meredith slipped into her seat. "Jem Baldwin was coming straight toward us," she went on. She tried to thrust the car into gear, then remembered she needed to start the ignition first.

Oh, dear heavens...

She started the car, put it into DRIVE, then drove toward the Downhome Diner, although the way her heart was racing, a nearby hospital might be a better choice. Fried chicken and pecan tart won out, however, and as they drove through a pretty maze of historic buildings, she breathed easier.

"So we basically just ran out because Jem came back?" Meredith asked, and Julia nodded emphatically.

"A close call," she declared as she angled into a parking spot in a lot just up the road from the diner. "I got us out of there in the nick of time."

"Except I'd like to have seen his reaction," Meredith mused. Her next words brought Julia up short. "How he handled knowing that we now know what he knows, or how he interacted with Rebecca."

Of course. *Don't run from adversity. March toward it if you want to uncover information.* Julia sighed. "Know your enemy."

Meredith chuckled. "Well, he's not exactly the enemy, but yes. Know your competition. Don't be afraid to go toe to toe. Size them up and assess the situation. It's all part of the investigatory process," she explained. "And there's nothing like that first chance to get an impression of someone."

"I blew it."

"Well, kind of," Meredith teased as she climbed out of the car. "But if we're all looking for the same information, our paths are likely to cross again, right?"

Julia was about to reply when a soft voice interrupted their conversation. "Ladies, have you come for dinner too?"

"Maggie Lu, hey." Julia smiled at the older woman in her trim navy-blue and white lightweight dress. They'd met Maggie Lu while trying to uncover old secrets surrounding the historic plantation of the Bessets, another family who held their past close to their chests, like so many did. "It's so nice to see you," Julia told her. "If you're just coming in, have supper with us. Becca is coming over too."

"I would love the kindly company of you ladies. Eating alone wears one thin," Maggie Lu replied.

"Oh, it does," Meredith agreed, and she and Maggie Lu exchanged sympathetic looks.

"My Charlene told me that Maribelle has made fresh peach pie with some of Leopold's creamy vanilla ice cream on the side, and I just turned my back on my leftover meatloaf and headed this way," Maggie explained as they strolled down the tree-lined street. Leopold's was a locally famous ice cream shop not far from the diner, and Charlene loved to use locally sourced items to augment her menu. "Life is too short to ignore the tastes of a Georgia summer, is it not?" she asked as they approached the diner entrance. "And it's a convenience to have so many things close at hand. Great cooking, and Leopold's has the best ice cream known to man, I do believe. I am blessed."

"As are we," Julia told her, and meant it.

Maggie's life hadn't resounded with blessings. She'd lived a tough childhood, but she'd not only worked to succeed, she'd helped others as an elementary school teacher. Hundreds of children had been touched by this woman's warmth and wisdom over multiple decades.

"Mom, we tempted you over." Maggie Lu's daughter waved a quick greeting as the teenage hostess seated them in a back corner. Charlene had opened the restaurant a few years before to fulfill a lifelong dream of running her own place after working for others. "I was hoping we would. And Maribelle made a coconut cake that's melt-in-your-mouth delicious. I was going to drop off a slice later."

"You spoil me," Maggie Lu scolded, but the smile on her face set the scolding aside. "It's a pleasure to have a daughter close by but an even better one to have her close at hand with a delightful restaurant!"

Charlene and her mother exchanged smiles as the three women settled into the red vinyl retro-styled booth. Bright yellow walls decked with nostalgic history lightened the long, narrow restaurant. An old-fashioned counter faced the kitchen, and the counter was lined with red-topped silver stools. In the mornings the counter was filled with local retired men, a popular gathering spot that got them out of the house and out of their wives' hair for a while, hours spent solving the problems of the world. The counter seats weren't as full right now, but the old-time feel of the place pervaded. The cook calling out orders, the waitresses posting tickets on a suspended carousel, and the smell of fried chicken filling the air like a Southern summer picnic.

"I love this place," Julia told Maggie Lu. "My husband used to take me to fancy places. He had it in his head that the higher the price and the more notable the chef, the better it was, but this right here is my kind of place. My kind of people," Julia went on. "It took Beau a little while to realize that simple is best. A triple bypass provided just enough convincing for him to re-embrace the everyday things in life. And coming here is like being a kid again, going to the little local restaurant with my grandpa holding my hand and how he'd lift me up and set me on one of those twisting stools and let me spin."

"Funny, how those things from childhood come back unexpectedly." Maggie took a napkin and unfolded it over her lap. "I think back to the trials and troubles and tragedies that abounded at times, but mostly I put all that aside and say 'Well then.' And I move on. But I pull the joyful moments close to my heart, they are that momentous. Life gives us turns and twists, but we walk the path we're given, don't we, now?"

"We surely do," Meredith agreed. "And when the hills are steep or the curves are sharp, we just keep on moving. For the Lord is our strength—"

"And our shield," Julia added. "When I faced things in the courtroom that had no sense or reason, when I saw children who'd so gravely lost their way as to never find it again, I remembered that verse, how even the most lost among us gains strength in the Lord."

"A prayin' judge is a fine thing to ponder," noted Maggie Lu as Tara approached their table with tall glasses of water. "And Miss Tara, if you would bring me some lemon for this water, I'd be most obliged."

"Have it right here, Mrs. King," Tara told her. She slipped a small plate of sliced lemons onto the table. "I heard y'all were waitin' on one more?"

"Rebecca's coming along in a few," Julia told her.

"Then how about a round of sweet tea? Unless you'd prefer somethin' else?" she drawled intentionally, as if wanting something else was against the law.

Julia laughed. "If you could bring me a Diet Dr Pepper, I'd appreciate it, Tara. Much as I like sweet tea, right now I'd prefer something carbonated."

"And this establishment will not hold it against you," Tara teased. She hurried away as Rebecca came through the diner door. Their new library friend glanced left and right and behind, as if expecting to be followed, and when she sank into the seat alongside Meredith, she groaned.

"You left me to sweep up the pieces." She laid her head back as if bested, then brought it right up and nailed Julia with a sharp look. "Jem Baldwin was quite upset that anyone else would choose to use that particular computer, and even more upset that I couldn't reinstate his browsing history. When I very kindly inquired as to why a famous author like him didn't use his own computer, he just glared at me—"

"You outed him?"

"I did. I don't care how rich and famous you are, if you come play on my turf, you play by my rules," Rebecca declared. She shoved a lock of light brown hair aside, hair that was just beginning to turn silver here and there. "And you wouldn't believe how his expression changed. And his attitude right along with it," she went on. "Quite the heads-up, if you know what I mean."

"Well, if Jem Baldwin is determined to dig up any and all information about the Greens, he could at least be nice while he's doing it."

"Bein' nice is important to us humans, isn't it?" asked Maggie Lu with a hint of *tsk-tsk* in her tone. "By very virtue of being human, we should be nice, but I am not one bit surprised that someone is looking to do a story on the Green family. Such a nice bunch of folks to go through so very much."

Julia's ears perked up.

From the quick lift of Meredith's chin, she saw that Maggie Lu had gotten her attention too. "You know the Greens, Maggie Lu?"

"Well, not personally, mind you, but anyone from this area knew *of* the Greens, of their good times and their bad times."

Bad times?

Julia leaned forward.

So did Meredith. "They had bad times?"

"Oh, child, anyone who lived through world wars and the Great Depression had bad times. Bein' rich didn't insulate one from the sorrows of the day. Granny Luv said that miscarrying two baby boys nearly put Mrs. Green over the top, and they were that worried about her that they looked at hospitalization, but a woman who loses two babies back-to-back like that is filled with sorrow. And guilt," she added firmly, "although there is no guilt involved, but you can't tell a mama that. No, ma'am."

"She lost two sons?" Meredith posed the question gently.

"Granny said she wanted a boy in the worst way. Yearnin', she called it, as if she just needed to have herself a baby boy to even out the family," Maggie Lu continued. "But she was great with child twice after giving birth to Bertha, and each time the child was lost. Two baby boys that never took a breath on earth. Granny said it about did her in, and it was years before she seemed to be herself again. Granny worked at the house next door for a bit, and whenever the Greens or their children were featured in the papers for doing this, that, or something else, she'd talk about Mr. and Mrs. Green like they were old friends, because that's how folks felt about them, she'd say. Like they were just regular folks, friends with everyone."

Julia silently blessed the day they'd met Maggie Lu King. She was a living, breathing history lesson in the kindest of ways. "Later, Granny Luv began sewing for this one or that since more women were working jobs or raising babies, and there weren't a lot of seamstresses working in the city. She saw opportunity and grabbed on tight. She was good with a needle and better with a machine. Sweet peach blossoms, that woman could sew a straight line with nary a pin, and it was a sight to see, even when she was getting on in years. She'd tell me stories about the soldiers she helped and how she would mend uniforms and send them back out to the troops. Once the U-boats were gone, of course."

U-boats. War efforts. "You've seen so much, Maggie Lu." Thinking of what the last century had brought, Julia sat back, amazed.

"Too much, some days," Maggie Lu told her. "Not enough on others, but a good memory and a talkin' Granny have served me well. Still, I look back and bless the opportunities that came my way. Better that than cursing the bad. I wasn't afraid to work against the wrongdoings, once I was of a more mature age, but Granny always said, 'Girl, don't get bogged down. Speak out when you can, but keep moving forward.' That's a lesson I learned at her knee," she finished as Tara returned to take their order.

Two babies lost.

The sadness on Patrice Green's face.

Were those things related? They certainly could be.

By the time they finished dinner, the conversation had shifted to strained air-conditioning units, the high cost of repairs, and troubled souls in Forsythe Park, but Julia couldn't wait to talk to Meredith alone.

Had Maggie Lu opened up a new avenue of exploration? Or just brought forward sad old news from a time when so many babies were lost before birth?

She didn't know, but she was pretty sure of one thing: Patrice Green's life may have been gilt-edged, but the sharp knife of sorrow had tarnished that edge, and that was something any woman could empathize with.

Chapter Six

"I AM NOT SPITTIN' INTO that thing. No way, no how." Harlowe Green folded his thin arms over his narrow chest and glowered at Meredith and Julia the next morning when Meredith handed him the small vial to collect his DNA sample. "I don't trust them things, not one bit."

Julia bit her tongue.

She was pretty sure the centenarian wouldn't appreciate a courtroom-style tongue-lashing, so she stayed mum while Meredith took the lead.

"Harlowe." Meredith kept her tone low and slow. She gave the elderly man a look like a mama would offer an errant child. "You did hire us to find Lawrence, correct?"

"Well, yes," he admitted and had the common sense to sound a little sheepish. He noted the four books of photographs with a jut of his chin. "Which is why I'm giving you our family pictures. But I thought you'd leave me out of it."

Meredith deepened the expression. "Harlowe, you are part of his family. You know that's an impossible expectation." Then she shushed up and waited.

That's where Julia would have messed up, because hushing and patience weren't exactly her strong suit, and she was just about to push the old fellow along with fairly strong encouragement, when he sighed. "Give me the thingamabob."

"Two," Meredith told him. She handed him the first little tube. "We're registering with two different genealogy sites to cover more ground."

"Ain't these things pricey?" he asked in a gruff tone, but he took the apparatus from her hand. "And I was told never to spit in front of a lady. Much less two," he grumbled, but when Meredith frowned, he got down to business. It took him a few minutes, but when he finished with the first sample, he didn't fuss when Meredith handed him the second tube.

Julia capped the first one and slipped it into the self-sealing envelope, then into the return shipping box. And when Harlowe had finished with the second one, she did the same thing.

"Thank you, Harlowe." Meredith stood and patted the elderly gentleman on the shoulder. "It's so much easier to build a puzzle if we have all the pieces."

"But if we lost Lawrence so long ago, he wouldn't be around to do this kind of business." He aimed a frown at the two ready-to-mail DNA kits. "So that doesn't make a lick of sense, does it?"

"On the contrary," Julia replied. "If Lawrence had any kind of offspring, the tests will identify them for us if they've registered."

"Lots of folks do this?" he asked, surprised.

"A great many," Meredith assured him, and she was just about to ask him another question when the doorbell interrupted them.

"Myla will shoo them off," he told them. "I don't entertain visitors without an appointment these days, as most folks are a waste of time. Mine and theirs, and when you don't have much time left, wasting it's the last thing I intend to do." As he stopped talking, hurried footsteps came their way.

"I told him you were busy, sir, but he busted on through and said 'I have an appointment,' even though he does not have any such thing." Myla Thomas wasn't a small woman, and she didn't shrink back for anything or anyone.

"You." Jem Baldwin stopped short and locked eyes with Julia. "You were at the library yesterday."

Cool as a cucumber, she stood and held his gaze just as firmly. "I certainly was."

"And my search history in the library system was conveniently erased by someone in the short space of time I was gone."

"If one leaves a search history on a public device, one shouldn't be surprised by whatever happens to it," Julia replied in a voice that would have done every Southern woman proud. "The words *public access* are fairly understandable, I believe."

"Except there was almost no one there when I left to make a couple of important calls, and when I came back, there you were." The author folded his arms across his chest. "And my search history was gone."

Meredith stood now too. "I wiped the history when I was done using the computer," she told him. "I always do that on a public computer. Isn't that the safe thing to do?"

He put a hand to his forehead, then dropped it and sighed. "Let me begin again." He sent Harlowe a look of compassion that surprised Julia. "My name is Jem Baldwin."

"One of the few authors who uses a current picture on his work so as to be recognizable," Julia noted, and when he smiled, she liked him a little bit better.

"It's an industry-wide thing to pretend that aging doesn't exist," he admitted. "May I sit down, sir?"

Myla huffed, but Harlowe waved her off. "We'll let him have his say, Myla. And thank you for looking out for me."

Myla fixed a fierce look at Jem. She said nothing but didn't have to. Her expression was enough of a reminder that Myla ruled the roost. She'd been taking care of Harlowe for nearly two decades, and she was clearly protective of her aged employer.

She turned on her heel and left them to face one another.

Harlowe wasted no time. "I hired these women."

"To mess with my research?" Jem seemed genuinely surprised. "Are you that against the idea of my story, sir?"

The fact that he called Harlowe "sir" softened Meredith's expression, but Julia wasn't so easily swayed. "I think there are a lot of families who might balk at the idea of opening too many closet doors, don't you?"

Jem didn't hurry his answer, and that won him another point. She didn't like people to be too glib in her courtroom, and she carried that into everyday life. Self-assuredness was fine, but quick talkers always made her do a thorough look at circumstantial evidence.

"There's always a surprise, isn't there?" He posed the question almost philosophically. "And then the urge to rush forward with the facts has to be weighed against collateral damage. Are you going to hurt people unnecessarily or damage otherwise pristine reputations?

Is the skeleton important enough to be unveiled? You might be surprised at how many old facts I don't use in my stories, or use in unrelated stories so nothing gets traced back."

"So you could take a fact from someone else's history and apply it to the story you're writing about the Greens?" Meredith's eyebrows shot up. "That's flagrantly dishonest."

"It's not," he assured her. "I write fiction. Yes, I use historical facts and characters to build the present-day conflict, but it's often a compilation. Mr. Green's family caught my attention because of the ongoing work his parents did for the community. Their kindness and largesse. They weren't rich initially, but clever choices and investing made Sully Green a wealthy man, and yet he never held his riches to his chest. My research shows that he and Patrice shared their good fortune with others, no matter their station in life. The rarity of that made me want to read more. So I did. And I saw a family filled with joy and sorrow," he added softly as he met Harlowe's gaze. "My research shows that your mama suffered from bouts of depression, and that was a difficult thing for a family to deal with. No one spoke of mental illness back then."

"Unless one was tetched in the head," agreed Harlowe, and Julia wasn't sure if he deliberately butchered the word or not. "But my mama wasn't sick, not one bit, and you can't be goin' around sayin' otherwise. She was a good woman who worked hard. She had rough spells, now and again." He looked defiantly at Jem. "Both of my parents were good people."

"Exactly why I picked them and your family to explore." Jem splayed his hands. "Not to get in your way or uncover secrets…"

Harlowe shot a very obvious guilt-filled look at the two women, practically shouting that he had things to hide.

"But to shed light on a tangled time in history, because that past can still trip up the present, and it's better if we all learn from the mistakes back then," Jem finished.

"Mr. Baldwin."

The author shifted his attention straight to Julia. She indicated Meredith with a thrust of her chin. "My friend has read all of your books. As have I."

"I sense a 'but' coming," he noted.

"While disseminating families in a fictional novel and thinly disguising historical threads that can easily be traced via today's technological devices can be riveting for the standard reader, research on a book could have devastating effects on a family's reputation. Consider what happened to the Windemere family after your blockbuster released in print and as a TV miniseries." The Windemeres had suffered grave financial losses via lawsuits filed against them when it turned out that the mid-twentieth-century patriarch had ordered the murders of two people who stood in his way of taking over significant parts of the shipping rail industry before the creation of the interstate system. "I'm not disputing the accuracy of that investigation, nor maligning the outcome, but you have to see that innocent people may suffer from the fallout of past wrongs."

"Although I was happy to see the Nimiipuu nation receive a substantial government compensation for your work on *Fight No More Forever*," noted Meredith. "But that didn't target an individual family," she explained. "It focused on military action run amok. Whereas your research here could affect a man and the offspring of Patrice and Sully who've done nothing wrong."

"So you have reason to believe Sully and Patrice did something wrong?" He honed in on her phrasing. He raised his hands. "Is there something you don't want me to find out?"

"Isn't there always?" Meredith leveled a calm but concerned look his way. "Harlowe's advanced years and his position in the community make us a little protective of him."

"I hear you." He studied Harlowe for a moment, then flexed his hands. "I will tread lightly. And if I find alarming circumstances, I can't promise I won't use them, but I can promise to be open and up front with you about them. You have my word." He extended his hand to Julia.

She accepted the gesture.

Then he did the same to Meredith. She fixed him with a look that rivaled the one she'd given Harlowe a quarter hour before. Meredith did that strict mama act real well. "When I take people at their word, it is with a mind of conviction and a healthy grain of salt. And I don't take to being disappointed, Mr. Baldwin. In any way, shape, or form."

"Jem," he told her. "Please. And I don't intend to disappoint anyone."

Julia wasn't so sure on that. Merely hunting up the past could open unsavory doors.

"Then we understand one another." Meredith gave his hand a quick shake. "And I think we've tired Harlowe out enough for the moment."

Jem took the cue. "Agreed. Mr. Green, I'll keep you apprised as needed."

"I don't get much say in it anyways, so it doesn't much matter, does it?"

"History being what it is, maybe not, but perhaps we'll find things to smile about. There's always that possibility."

Harlowe's face softened. "My parents were good people, so I think you'll find plenty that's good. But I've been around a long time, and there was bad all around us for a lot of years. And there's my worry."

"Well, sometimes bad begets more bad, and sometimes it makes others rise above and do the right thing. Maybe we'll find both, Mr. Green." Jem moved toward the door. "I'll be in touch."

"And we'll talk to you soon, Harlowe." Meredith hurried toward the door behind Jem, and when Julia got there, she saw Meredith zooming in on Jem's car for a few quick pictures.

"I'd never have thought of that," muttered Julia, balancing the heavy photo books in her arms. "Dashing out here to grab a picture."

"Saves us wondering and having to look things up later," Meredith told her. "It's a rental, but if we see it, we'll know we're following a similar track."

"You are good at this." Julia set the DNA kits in the trunk and swiped a hanky across her forehead lightly.

"I was somewhat immersed in it for nearly forty years, so proximity helps. But your experience with examining evidence and seeing folks' reactions and questioning their time, their motives, well…" Meredith slipped her phone back into the pocket of her capris and shrugged. "That's huge, Julia. Put them both together—"

"And we make a great team."

"Exactly. Now." Meredith put her signature sunglasses firmly into place. "Let's mail those kits and see what Carmen's found. She's texted me six times."

"I've got eight." Julia held up her phone for Meredith to see. "And one of them says she's making flan, so I may rethink this whole notion of working in an off-site office when we can get gourmet desserts if we keep Carmen busy in the kitchen."

Meredith laughed. "Don't worry, I've got plans for that old kitchen at the agency, when we can get Arnold to finish fixing your ceiling. And if baking tides her over until we make some more money and have more clients, it's a wonderful reward for all of us."

Dodgeville, Wisconsin
Spring 1931

Mrs. Hans Engstrom.
A new look.
A new name.
A new job.
And a new love. She'd been so certain, so absolutely certain that a new life would wipe the slate clean.
And it still wasn't enough. Never enough. Not for a dog-tired soul that hid an awful truth.

"Carrie."

She turned and tried to wipe the raw emotions from her face, but Hans knew. He always did.

"A bad day?"

"No." She tried to put a firm hold on her rising emotions. "Well, yes. But it will pass, Hans. It always does."

A mix of compassion and concern vied for his dear features. "You're not sick?"

The morning sickness had pretty much passed. "It's better now. Like your mother said."

"You need to rest more. I can take on more of the work here." He indicated the little house set beneath a copse of trees on the northeast corner of the Engstrom dairy farm in central Wisconsin. "And you need to leave the cheese factory, Carrie."

A discussion they'd had many times the past few weeks. She understood her dear husband's need to provide for her. For their baby. Hans was a good man, a strong Christian, and a good provider, but she couldn't stay home, waiting for days to pass.

Maybe this baby would be the turning point. Maybe being a mother, having a child of her own, would push aside the gaping hole that never seemed to be filled. Of course it would, because holding her own baby, leading her own life, would offset those old feelings that rose up like the ocean waves on those summer vacations along the coast of Maine. That image alone was enough to make her short of breath. Was that where they lost that beloved *child? Did they fail to watch him? Did he venture too close to the cliffs? Or—*

She couldn't begin to think of the "or." Every time she did, she wondered if her silence left her party to a crime.

Patrice in a bad frame of mind.

Lawrence, disinclined to listen and loving the center of attention, a fearless child who embraced his scant years with wild child abandon, but when Patrice was unwell, Lawrence's antics got on her nerves.

Don't think of it.

She tried not to, but when the summer heat built in Wisconsin, she thought of that one fateful vacation, a vacation without her to watch the boys, that changed everything. And her heart couldn't seem to bear it. "I like my job, and the Linzers are a good family to work for. It will be different when the baby's here, but I need to keep busy, Hans. You know that."

"My mother is busy enough, she could use your help," he reminded her, but the thought of his mother, watching her every move, dogging her every step, seemed prohibitive.

"When our little one is here, I will be here. For now I'll work like I've always done. Please don't press it, Hans." She met his kind but firm gaze with a direct look of her own. "You understood this when we married. What has changed?" He hesitated, and she sighed. "Your mother is telling you that a woman should stay home. Especially a woman in a delicate condition."

"Propriety has always been our way. My parents brought that mindset when they came here. It was that way in Europe. And it's not a bad thing to adopt here. Is it?"

How to answer him and not cause offense? She sighed softly. "Propriety is not always about appearances, my love. Sometimes it is about control, and I am determined to set my own course. That's not a bad thing, Hans."

And yet his expression indicated it wasn't necessarily a good thing, either. He reached out. Drew her in. Held her. "I would like to chase the old thoughts away. Leave you only room for new thoughts, liebchen. For me. For us. For our child."

How she wished he could do just that, but for ten years she'd carried those soul-stealing secrets with her. Could she tell him? Did she dare?

No.

He would insist on going to the law, and what would that bring upon them? Havoc. Pure havoc. Whatever happened on that northern excursion, it couldn't have been deliberate. Could it? And yet the thought that it might have been still kept her up at night. Especially in July.

Chapter Seven

"I HAVE NEVER HAD A better flan, and I mean that with all my heart. Missing lunch has absolutely nothing to do with my assessment." Julia swiped another small plate of warm flan from the countertop. "And to consider this lunch, I really need two servings. With my coffee."

"You really like it." Carmen smiled as she noted their looks of appreciation. "You're not just saying it, right?"

"Have I ever done that?" Julia asked dryly, and Carmen shook her head.

"Not where I'm concerned. Okay, while you eat, let me fill you in on a couple of things."

"We're listening." Meredith sighed as she finished the last bite from her second dish. "I inhaled that, and my diet coach will not be pleased, and I'll have to put in a whole lot of extra steps today," she said, then paused, one hand held up. "Wait, first tell us about your night with Harmony. How did it go?"

"Wonderful." Carmen's smile deepened and a look of satisfaction softened her big brown eyes. "We got chicken nuggets and fries—"

"Carmen for the win!" laughed Meredith.

"Keepin' it simple." Carmen retrieved printouts from the counter behind her. "Then the playground, and a walk along the water. She loves the birds, and she about came unglued when we spotted a pair of wood storks."

"They're like half vulture, half stork," Julia said. "We see them occasionally by us, and they're huge."

"She was mesmerized," Carmen noted. "She couldn't stop talking about it. We bought ice cream that melted instantly, so that was a mess."

"Oh, Carmen, I remember that so well." Meredith winced. "The boys always wanted to eat theirs outside, and it was like mush in sixty seconds at our temperatures. In the spring and fall it's fine, but summertime in Georgia has a fast and cruel effect on ice cream. Did you ever hear of Woody Pond?" she asked as Carmen sorted papers onto the counter. When Carmen shook her head, Meredith continued. "It's the greatest thing for wood storks. They developed a rookery about fifty miles south, less than an hour's drive with the highways, and there are hundreds of wood storks there. Babies, mamas, papas. They literally saved the stork by developing this rookery about thirty years ago. I bet your little friend would love a trip down there."

"It smells like an aviary," warned Julia. "Beau insisted we go there about eight years back. The birds were amazing, but hundreds of birds produce a lot of dung, and once was enough for me. But Harmony would never forget the sight," she finished as she accepted the printout from Carmen. "What have we here?"

"Some shots of the Green family from random internet pages. I looked for obscure sites because I wanted to pull up pictures that weren't in the mainstream papers. There weren't a ton, of course, but there were more than we would have found for a regular family from back then, because the Greens were always reaching out to others."

"Harlowe gave us photo books too."

"Except the little boy you're looking for isn't in them," noted Carmen practically.

"Did you see him in the online pictures?" asked Meredith.

Carmen shook her head. "Nothing. But if you've got Harlowe's pictures, we could do comparisons and see who shows up in both."

Julia hated to spoil their enthusiasm, but her practical nature jumped in. "We're talking nearly a century ago, with pictures that are also that old. That's a lot of dead people, ladies." She hated to add that last, but facts were facts.

"All true, but sometimes the leanest clues give the best results." Meredith rinsed her plate and slipped it into the dishwasher. "Let's spread out on the table. We can each take a pile of pictures and a book and study them. We'll need coffee," she added.

"I'm on it." Carmen took the printouts to the table. "I've sent you links to other pages, but these were pictures that had clear images of household help, the nanny, then another nanny, gardeners, and the people Sully worked with."

Julia had never been a "search for the needle in a haystack" kind of woman, but as she studied the photos with a magnifying glass, she developed a greater respect for the work of police investigators. Her neck ached, and she was pretty much cross-eyed two hours later. And she needed more coffee. She was just about to get some when she flipped a page of the third family photo book. She looked at the book, then the newspaper clipping, then the book again. "What year did Lawrence disappear?"

"Around 1921 we think, right? If Harlowe was five years old and Lawrence was four years old, it should be around there, since Harlowe was born in 1916."

"And this nanny is in this 1921 picture, and in several of these family photos in the book. And then she's gone in this October 1921 picture, and the new nanny's name is Nancy Lee MacArthur."

"Nanny Nancy." Meredith frowned. "A fairly awful title pairing. But other than that, why do we care? I think nannies and household help went on to other jobs and positions all the time back then, didn't they?"

"Sure, but who includes a nanny in a wide share of family pictures?" Julia asked. "This first nanny is in a lot of these casual pictures of Harlowe and his sisters. Check this out." She withdrew the printouts that included the nanny. "Here they're playing at the beach, going to the fair, and riding the pony. And there was one back here…" Julia flipped back through page after page of old pictures, then paused. She reached in, carefully withdrew a picture, and handed it to Meredith. Apparently curious, Carmen came and looked over Meredith's shoulder. When she noticed the image, she whistled softly. "That's Patrice with the nanny?"

"Yes. She's identified as Carolina Lambert on the back of one of the other pics, but yes. She's the nanny. Notice anything about the two women?"

"They look like best friends." Meredith flipped the picture over. The back was blank, not unusual for folks who were busy raising children. "You're sure this is the nanny?"

"One hundred percent. She's identified in a newspaper clipping that Carmen pulled off the internet. So they clearly have some kind of relationship here." Julia pointed toward the picture in Meredith's hands. "And she's obviously a big part of their lives. She's with them and the children on vacation, in the park, and at home, so why does she get replaced a few months after Lawrence disappears?"

"It could be coincidence." Carmen tapped a finger to the table. "But not likely."

"How's that?" asked Meredith, and Julia silently commended her. She hadn't been sure how Meredith would handle Carmen's straightforward outspokenness, and the way she wasn't afraid to butt in as needed. Meredith didn't know the full extent of Carmen's past and her narrow scrapes with the law as a teenager.

Julia did. That's how they came to be friends, and if ever a kid needed a friend and a mentor, it was Carmen back then.

"When a family includes hired help in so many pictures, it says acceptance. It's a gesture of inclusiveness that goes beyond employer and employee."

"And looking ahead to the next few years, I only see two pictures of Nanny Nancy with the children. One on a summer vacation in Maine where a news photographer got a shot, and then this one at Christmas in 1929." Meredith tapped a photo of the children with their nanny.

"The first Depression Christmas," noted Julia.

"And Patrice is nowhere to be seen in these 1929 pictures, but we have her later in the book."

"And then another several pages with no images of Patrice before 1934," Julia added. "Except for the one at the ribbon-cutting ceremony where she looked so sad." Julia slid that photo out for Carmen to see. "Maggie Lu told us that Patrice had suffered two miscarriages."

"Two boys," Meredith told Carmen. "Could these blank spots coincide with those losses? The depression of loss and postpartum hormones?"

"Either is enough to wreak havoc," said Julia. "I've never had a child, but I've seen cases of postpartum depression in my court-room, and they were tragic."

"I expect they were." Meredith hesitated, then took a deep breath. "We miscarried once, between the boys," she said to Carmen. "I was devastated. I'm sure Ron was too, but being a man with a job, he just kept working and working. For me, it was like every day gaped open. I had Carter, and that was a blessing. He kept me busy. But that first year I couldn't stop thinking of that due date, and how excited I'd been. I dreaded it coming, and I thought Ron would dread it too, but he was on a case, and it just kind of slipped by. He didn't mention it until days afterward. Not an after-thought, exactly, but not something he dwelled on, either. Whereas I couldn't get that wretched date out of my mind no matter what I did." She fingered the picture of Patrice, remembering. "It seemed to take forever for me to get pregnant again after that. We finally went for treatments, and that's how I got Chase and why the boys are ten years apart."

"Those things weigh hard on a woman," noted Julia. "And there's so little others can do to help." She understood that well. Ovarian cysts had kept her from ever conceiving. It was sad then, but years had softened the blow of never having children. And God had blessed her by letting her help hundreds of children through the court processes.

"Having the love of friends helped," said Meredith. "I wonder if Patrice had any good friends. It's kind of odd that you never see her with friends, isn't it?"

"Maybe not for those times," said Carmen. "I don't think people were snapping shots like they do now. Of absolutely everything. Including food. It's ridiculous."

"You're right, photographs were special." Meredith's brows drew down. "I wish I could remember where exactly I saw that similar cardboard frame Harlowe had around Lawrence's picture."

"Which brings us back to how he managed to find and keep a picture of a child whose pictures were wiped off the map nearly a hundred years ago, Meredith." Julia planted her elbows on the table and leaned forward. "Does he know more than he's telling us? Because it's not normal for a five-year-old to be astute enough to squirrel away a picture and keep it. If he were older, sure. But not at age five."

"Have you ladies considered this might be his cry for help?" asked Carmen. "That maybe he's the one with a guilty conscience? It makes sense, doesn't it? The author coming around out of the blue and digging up scraps, then Harlowe seeking you out. Maybe if he's going to get caught in something wrong, an accident or something, he wants it to be discovered by friends. Not foes."

"You think he could be purging himself." Julia hated that the thought made sense.

"I think people of faith want to go home to God with a clear conscience," said Carmen. "If he did something that hurt his brother when they were little, the guilt may have never left. Not because a five-year-old is responsible," she added hastily. "He's not. But the guilt might be too much weight to bear at that age. And the thought of a book has stirred it all up."

"I can't deny that the thought has crossed my mind." Julia faced Meredith. "I know he's an old friend of yours, but I think we need to put Harlowe on the suspect side of things until we either clear him or find the truth." She breathed a sigh of relief when Meredith offered a brisk nod.

"I agree. This could be a cry for help, and we shouldn't overlook that. I'll rack my brain about that photo sleeve too, but in the meantime, have we identified any of these folks in these old pictures?"

"Some have names. Many don't. But by cross-referencing them, we should be able to match up some, don't you think?"

"I'll get on that," said Carmen. "That's something I can easily do right here while you ladies look for other things. With Harlowe's siblings gone, it's tough, but they all have middle-aged grandchildren. They might know more than you think."

"We might have a history buff among them."

"There are thirteen grandchildren," noted Julia. "Wilma's family has eight. Bertha's has five. Let's start there. If we put together a list of addresses—"

"Done." Carmen slipped them each a copy of all thirteen grandchildren. "Names, spouses, addresses, and some emails. Also house phones. Amazing what you find on the web, isn't it?"

"I say we contact them right now," Julia said. "If anyone's available today, we go see them."

Meredith held up her hand. "Or we simply drop in and surprise them. You know that first expression of dread, confusion, or surprise is a quick study."

"I like how she thinks." Carmen grinned as she moved back to the kitchen. "Don't let the left hand know what the right hand's doing. On the right side of the law, that is," she added with a wink toward Julia.

"So we just show up? Unannounced?"

"Welcome to Investigations 101." Meredith slung her purse over her shoulder. "Let's go while we've got surprise on our side. There are seven of them in Georgia, five in the Savannah area. Let's see what they've got. Shall we?"

Julia grabbed her bag. "I've been listening to fish stories for the four weeks that Beau was home. While I like fish just fine, diving into surprise attacks sounds infinitely more exciting. See you later, Carmen."

"Have fun. And be careful," she called after them.

Julia accepted the warning.

Not that any of these people were dangerous. Far from it. She hoped. But dropping in and delving into family history wasn't considered acceptable behavior in the South. And yet—

That was exactly what they were about to do.

Chapter Eight

"JULIA! I INTENDED TO CALL you today," Reverend Ed Markham called out as she and Meredith retreated from their fourth unsuccessful drop-in visit. Two of Harlowe's young relatives weren't at home, one shut the door in their faces, and this great-grandnephew happened to live in a quaint old home kitty-corner across the road from New Beginnings Church, the wonderful congregation she and Beau had stumbled upon about eight years back. Ed's love for people, open arms, sound doctrine, and great sense of humor had given them a home away from home, and Julia loved being part of his outreach ministries. They didn't do too many midsummer, but once school was back in session, it was all hands on deck.

Julia crossed the street and gave Ed a hug. "What's up? It can't be committee meeting time already? You know we all need a few months off, Ed," she teased.

He laughed as Meredith joined them then extended his hand toward her. "Ed Markham, pastor here." He motioned to the old church behind him.

"Meredith Bellefontaine, friend and business partner to her." Meredith hooked a thumb toward Julia after she shook Ed's hand.

"Business partner?" Ed raised a brow of interest toward Julia. "That sounds wonderful. Retirement works well for some but not all, and Julia's been chomping at the bit for the past few months," he noted. "Glad to hear you've jumped into something else. Sitting in a boat or walking a creek might work for Beau, but it's not the answer for everyone."

"It isn't, and I'm not a sit-at-home kind of gal, so working with Meredith is marvelous."

Ed faced Meredith. "Julia and Beau have been a gift to this congregation from the moment they stepped in the door our second year here. So are you canvassing the neighborhood?" He cast an amused look across the street. "Selling perfume? Encyclopedias? Brushes or vacuum cleaners?"

"I hate to admit that I remember my parents hearing all those door-to-door spiels when I was little." Julia laughed. "We wanted to see your neighbor there, but he didn't want to be seen."

"Alan Pierson." The pastor's expression sobered. "He's had his share of problems. Lost his wife. And his job. He's been reeling ever since. He doesn't go to church, doesn't talk to God, and barely talks to his children, although he's got one daughter, Delia, who refuses to give up. She says she doesn't care if depression runs in the family, she's not going to lose her father to it."

"She's a fighter."

"And a firm believer," added Ed. "What did you need to see Al for?"

"We're helping his great-uncle on an information quest and thought his sisters' grandkids might be able to share stories. Shed some light on things."

"Then you want Delia, not Al," Ed determined. "She's his youngest daughter. She's recently married, has no kids, and lives by the river. She married rich, but you'd never know it, because she's about the most humble gal I know."

"Do you have her address?" asked Julia.

"Naomi does, but she's running the girls to music lessons right now. They're part of that 'Summer in the Park' series, and the ensemble practices once a week together. That's why I was calling you," he said to Julia. "Several of our youth are involved, and I figured you'd want to know about it."

Julia had been helping as legal counsel and a youth group coordinator for the last several years. "I'll be sure to catch at least one of the concerts," she told him. "Can you have Naomi call me? Or text me if that's easier?" Naomi was the organizer in the family and the congregation. While Ed's heart was always in the right place and his hands were kept busy helping others, minor details like dates and times escaped him. The congregation liked to say that while Ed's counsel helped heal the heart, Naomi's practicality kept things running smooth. Together they were an amazing team, and the New Beginnings congregation loved them.

"Of course. You know Myla tried to get Al to come to New Beginnings. Proximity alone made us a convenient choice. She's known the family for a long time."

Julia nodded. So did Meredith.

"But Al shrugged her off. Said that God had given him enough sadness and sorrow, and he had no interest in seeking out more."

"Depression is a dreadful, draining thing," Meredith noted. "And this can't be easy on his daughter."

"No, but she's a feisty thing. Doesn't take no for an answer. Says that 'no' just means 'try harder.' And that's the attitude she takes with life."

"She's my kind of people," Julia declared, but she wondered if she would have that kind of fortitude and patience under similar circumstances. She'd like to think so, but her impatient nature might be her undoing. "I'll look forward to hearing from Naomi."

"I'll text her right now." He did too. They both knew that if he didn't, he'd be most likely lost in his musings on Sunday's readings and totally forget what he promised to do. "See you Sunday."

"He's so nice." Meredith clipped her seat belt into place once they got back into the car. "And I'll be excited to meet Delia. First, because I love that name. It made the short list if I ever had a girl, which I did not."

"Great name," agreed Julia.

"And I love to see younger people with an appreciation for history. You don't see much of that these days."

"We've got one last contact." Julia glanced at the dashboard clock. "But it's dinnertime for most folks. Do we dare interrupt dinner?"

"It might be the only way to find people at home. Is this Alan's brother?"

"His half brother."

"Let's do it."

Richard Pierson was nothing like his brother. He saw them coming up his fairly long walkway and met them halfway. "Ladies, hello." He held a pair of tongs in one hand and was wearing an apron that said GRILLIN' AND CHILLIN', and his smile underscored that mantra. "Can I help you?"

Julia introduced herself, then let Meredith take over. "Your great-uncle hired us to do some family research for him," she explained. "But it's hard to find one-hundred-year-old information when most everyone from that time is deceased."

"Uncle Harlowe is on a quest, hmm?" He motioned for them to follow him to the grill, where he flipped four burgers and the same number of bratwursts before he turned the fire down. "I like to simmer them at the end," he explained. He put the spatula down. "Your best bet is my niece, Delia. She's the history buff in the family, she got that trait. My brother loved history too, but he's been in a rough way for a while."

"We stopped there," Julia told him. "He seemed very sad."

Richard's expression sobered. "He's always been prone to that. As if he's carrying the weight of the world on his shoulders. He gets better for a while, but then life hits him crosswise, and he slips downhill again. My sister rails on him from Kentucky, telling him if he'd just find the right church, he'd be fine, and she won't leave it alone. I don't look at my brother and see his sadness as a lack of faith. It's more like something gets trip-wired in his brain, then keeps spinning. Did you know he was a history professor?"

The ladies shook their heads in unison. "American history?" asked Meredith.

Richard shook his head. "Infancy." He smiled. "That's what he says about American history. He says that four hundred years is like 'yesterday' in true history. No, he delved into the rise and fall of empires and how their mistakes and courage led to the world as we know it today. I'm no history buff, but when Al talked, people listened. He made it come alive. Delia got that from him. Let me text her that you two want someone to talk to. She's always happy to help. Funny how genes work, isn't it?" He texted a quick message as he spoke. "She looks like her mom and got her nature, but that love of history and family is Green, through and through."

"That's so nice of you." Meredith smiled as he hit SEND on the text. "And yes, genetics offers a real mix of things, doesn't it?"

His phone pinged back quickly. He read the text out loud. "'Tell them I'd be happy to talk. Come right over. Or we can talk over supper. Starving.'" His smile widened when he read that word, then he lifted his gaze to Meredith. "Give me your number, and we'll include you on the text, then you gals can make arrangements. I've got to get this meat inside before my children realize they haven't eaten in thirty minutes. More or less."

Meredith gave her number, and her phone pinged when she and Julia reached the car. "The diner?" she asked Julia as they got in.

Julia nodded. "No one else I'd rather give my business to."

"Fifteen minutes," Meredith announced after sending and receiving another text. "Her husband's coming too."

"Newlyweds."

"Ah, yes." Meredith smiled, but Julia saw a hint of sadness in her gaze. "I remember it well."

Julia adjusted her seat belt. "As we should. Life trips us up, but the getting on with life opens a lot of unseen doors."

"It does." Meredith nodded as Julia started the car and began driving to the restaurant. "But the house still seems to echo every night. Not sad, exactly. Just way too silent."

"Then you need a noisier cat. Or a squawking bird?"

"And drive GK to distraction?"

"Give the old boy something to be grumpy about, instead of just acting grumpy," Julia noted. "Although grumpy cats are a big deal these days."

"GK actually almost opened his eyes when I got home the other night," Meredith teased. She said it in jest, but Julia knew the truth of it. "Then he realized that was far too much trouble and kept right on sleeping." Meredith let the topic drop, but this wasn't the first time she'd mentioned the empty house yawning at night. Carter lived two hours away, and with a busy family, his visits weren't all that frequent. Chase was nearly twice that distance but made it a priority to visit at least once a month. He was an associate professor at Emory. Still, that left a lot of empty nights in the month, and Julia had no idea how to help that.

Tara seated them as soon as they got to the restaurant. Charlene waved from the kitchen. Julia and Meredith waved back. Tara slipped menus onto the table, then promptly came back with their drinks. "Diet Dr Pepper and sweet tea," she announced. "Lemon for the tea, and I thought a cherry would be nice for your drink, Judge." She smiled as she set them down. "This will get you started while you wait for your other two." She'd no sooner walked away than Jem Baldwin walked in the door. He glanced around, spotted them, and waved.

Julia waved back.

Meredith groaned, but as Jem approached their table, she mustered up an almost-real smile on her face. It only fell short by a mile or two.

"Ladies, a nice surprise."

"For us as well," noted Julia. She gave Meredith's calf a quick nudge with her toe.

"A long day, it's nearly seven thirty," he noted. Was he waiting for an invitation to join them? That would put a total kibosh on their conversation with Delia and her husband. "I want to apologize again if I came on too strong this morning."

"Apology accepted." Meredith kept her tone bright, but Julia couldn't miss the cool undertone.

Jem hesitated, as if he wanted to say more, but then Tara called out his name. "Mr. Baldwin?"

"Yes, ma'am." He acknowledged her with a quick wave, then dipped his chin toward Julia and Meredith. "I got supper to go."

"A working supper?" Julia asked.

He nodded. "That seems to be my schedule these past few years. I'm not sure if that's good or bad."

"A driven nature isn't a bad thing, but you're right," Julia told him. "It's easy to get too caught up in things and let life pass us by."

Emotion deepened his gaze. Not sadness, really. But not joy, either. "It is. I promised myself that wouldn't happen on this book, then promptly broke that promise."

"A focused nature isn't bad, is it?"

He met Julia's gaze. "No. And I hope I don't sound like I'm whining."

Meredith's light hum indicated she might actually be thinking that very thing.

He shifted his attention to her, then back to Julia. "I've been blessed with a career I love and money in the bank. But in the meantime

I let a lot of other parts of life slip away. I'm thirty-six years old, and I thought it would be different now."

Meredith had been gazing down at the table. She lifted her eyes and looked him square in the face. "It can only be different if you make different choices."

His forehead knit.

"That old theory of insanity, remember?"

His face relaxed. "Rita Mae Brown. One of my favorite mystery authors. Doing the same thing over and over again and expecting different results."

"Exactly. If you keep putting it off, eventually you're thirty-seven. Then forty. Then fifty. And you look back and wonder why you didn't hop off that merry-go-round years before."

He studied her for a few seconds. "You're right. A promise with no follow-through is just loose talk."

"Yes."

He looked at Meredith as if she'd given him something special, then backed away. "Wise words."

"Well." She sent him a genuine smile this time. And he smiled back, then went and paid for his dinner. As he left the restaurant, a young couple swung in.

Chapter Nine

JOY SURROUNDED THEM.

The young woman wore a classic fitted T-shirt and shorts that left long bare legs showing, while the heart-stoppingly good-looking fellow was in khaki shorts, a three-button pink golf shirt, and some kind of worn sandals. They paused, and when she flipped a smile over her shoulder at him, they were a perfect photo op for a young couple in love.

"Delia?" Meredith called softly.

"Yes." The young woman came their way, took a seat, and shook hands quickly. Her big, broad husband moved more slowly but seemed equally affable. "I'm so glad you had Uncle Rich text me." She folded her hands on the table and seemed utterly sincere. "I know Uncle Harlowe is up in arms over this book thing, and I hate to see him bothered at this stage of his life, but it is rather exciting, isn't it? To have your family history possibly be the basis for a book? Not too many folks can say that."

"True," said Julia.

"But if he's hired you, it's because he's scared," Delia declared. "And that's got me wondering why he's scared. It's not right to have a centenarian afraid of anything. Uncle Harlowe has been good to all of us over the years. His only son died in Korea and he's been alone since Auntie passed away twenty-four years ago, but he's a rare bird that keeps abreast of all that's going on in the family. He loves us," she finished simply. "So what's bothering him? If this book takes that dear, sweet man over the edge, I'll go have a talk with Jem Baldwin myself."

Julia picked her words carefully. "We're scouting for skeletons," she told them.

"We're not sure if there are any," added Meredith, "but your uncle decided that if any existed, he'd rather have us stumble onto them before Mr. Baldwin."

"That's Uncle in a nutshell," Delia told them. They paused the conversation when Tara stopped at their table to take their order. When she was done, Delia picked up right where she left off. A tribute to youth, Julia decided, that she didn't have to stop and think at all. "He's always one step ahead of the game. When you played chess with him, you realized real quick that he was already prepping the board for your third move to come, simply by experience and your personality."

"And he's never let me win. Not once," noted her husband. "I'm Jared."

Julia paused and looked at him again. Then she sighed. "Jared Johnson Junior? Triple J, the—"

"The NFL quarterback?" Meredith whispered. "Out of Florida? Who beat our Dawgs in two successive years playing college ball?"

He glanced around with a pretend look of chagrin, but there were only a handful of people in the restaurant at seven forty-five. "Guilty as charged. And thank you for not mentioning that twice we fell apart in the playoffs."

"Well, you've come back to the mother ship," Meredith noted, meaning that Triple J would now be leading the Atlanta Falcons on their quest for a new championship. "You're a hometown boy now, working for our side. I was at my husband's side for a lot of Georgia games, but those two crushing defeats—oh, it was a long ride home from Jacksonville, let me tell you."

"I can just imagine." Delia reached across the table and squeezed Jared's hand. "Winners hate losing, and it's never a fun night in our house when the team loses. But we've got great hopes for the next few years, don't we, Triple J?"

He groaned softly, and she laughed.

"We'll have plenty of time to talk football soon," she told the ladies. "It'll dominate my life from July fifth through February, but let's talk about Uncle Harlowe. I'm well versed in our family history. His great-great-great-grandfather was a Savannah slave trader. That's a family sorrow and common knowledge, but the family made its money in railroads and shipping, not the slave trade. The Broussard side of the family came down with the Acadian expulsion, and the Broussards were originally designated for South Carolina but ended up here. Janelle Broussard made French lace for some of Savannah's most elegant gowns, and her granddaughter Marie caught the eye of James Green. Her distaste for slavery had James turn his eye toward westward expansion, and he made a fortune by investing in railroads, then shipyards. His timing was spot-on. He was fond of saying 'own nothing, control everything.'"

"Middleman philosophy."

"Yes. They survived the War Between the States with everything intact, thanks to General Sherman's admiration for the city, but a good share of the fortune was lost then rebuilt as shipping and rail expanded west and into international trade. But in all of that, I've found no family scandals except for a couple of cheating husbands, which will not become the norm. Right, darling?" She batted her pretty eyelashes across the table, and Jared laughed.

"Absolutely right. I'm happy right where I am, my love."

"As am I."

Oh, the look she gave him. A look of such love and tenderness that Julia didn't dare glance toward Meredith, because she was sure her friend would be misty-eyed. Fortunately Tara arrived with bowls of gumbo, and it was hard to find anything too sentimental about great soup. But when the soup was done and they were waiting for their sandwiches, Julia probed again. "Since you're the family expert, what can you tell us about the twentieth-century Greens? Harlowe's parents. Their kids."

"Oddly enough, not as much as I can about the earlier ancestors in some ways. I mean, their lives are out there, it was a time of print and acquisition, and Sullivan Green wasn't afraid to make things happen. He was on several boards, he was a hospital overseer, he was well respected everywhere. I think my great-great-grandmother was your more typical 'stand by my man' wife. You don't see her as much. You don't hear about her as much."

"And yet I've seen reports that they did everything together," Meredith prodded with a tiny frown. "That he loved her amazingly."

"I believe that's true," Delia replied. "But seeing someone in newspaper and periodical shots isn't the same as knowing them, if you know what I mean. Everyone knew Sully Green. But Patrice seemed to have her good times and bad times, and I think that was a problem. A problem my dad still faces today."

"Depression."

Delia's expression saddened. "It's a hard thing to deal with. Hard to fight. My dad gets better until something knocks him down again. Losing my mom just put him over the edge, and he's been sad ever since. I don't know how to help him."

"We pray," Jared told her. "We keep communication open, and we pray."

"Good-looking and smart," Meredith declared softly. She put her hand on Delia's. "I've found that reading about loss doesn't help most people, because we're all individuals. Folks talk about the first anniversary, the first Christmas, the first everything. What they forget to mention is that sometimes the third and the fourth are just as hard. That there is no timeline on grief, and we all feel it differently."

"It can last that long?" Delia lifted both brows in surprise.

"It doesn't have to," Julia told her. "Although I still get misty-eyed when I hear big band music because it reminds me of my father, who was a huge fan. He used to dance us around the kitchen to Glenn Miller music. We lost him in a tragic car accident nearly fifteen years ago, but I still get emotional when I hear the opening strains of those old songs. In a sensitive soul like your father, even those later anniversaries can trigger emotion. I think you're both doing the right thing," she finished as Tara approached with four of Charlene's amazing Savannah burgers, a mouthwatering concoction of seasoned beef, coleslaw, secret sauce, and melted cheese. "Keep up the prayers, and keep him involved. And treat him normally," she added. "Nobody likes to think they're abnormal, right?"

Delia exchanged a rueful look with Jared. "I've been doing the exact opposite, I'm afraid."

"Because you love him."

She nodded. "But you're probably right, my concern makes him feel like there's something wrong. I think it reminds him."

"Can't hurt to try, can it?" admitted Jared. His eyes lit up at the sight of the burgers, and when he'd taken his first bite, he positively groaned in happiness. "This has got to be the best burger I've ever eaten in Savannah or anywhere else. Babe, can you—"

She didn't even let him finish. She picked up her phone, snapped a picture, and posted it to social media. "Done and tagged to you and the diner. The world now knows that you break diet protocol now and again."

"A man's got to eat," he told her, and when he grinned, Julia had no problem seeing the same charisma she'd noted during postgame interviews.

Delia picked up her phone between bites. Julia was drawing the opinion that it was rude, when Delia stopped typing after she'd eaten about half of her food. "I'm texting you some tidbits," she told Meredith when she finally set the phone down. A series of pings indicated that Meredith's phone had received them. "We've got to meet some friends at nine, and I didn't want to cut this short. I'll message you a few links that might be helpful, but with all my research over the years, I've never uncovered anything of great concern. That makes me think that Uncle Harlowe's worries will go unfounded."

"Thank you." Meredith patted her phone. "We're absolutely appreciative. And would you guys mind if we took a picture?" she added. "My sons are not going to believe I had dinner with Triple J without proof."

"I'd love it," Jared declared. He got up out of his seat, came around behind the ladies, and snapped a selfie that looked great.

"That came out awesome!" exclaimed Meredith, laughing. "My nose always looks so big when I do it."

"Long arms help," he told them. "Ladies, thank you for getting ahold of us."

"Yes," Delia added as she slung a cute purse over her shoulder. "I'm glad Uncle reached out to you, and I'm super grateful for your advice about Dad. Normal and patient. Got it."

When Tara came along to pick up plates a few minutes later, Julia asked her for the check.

Tara sighed and hooked her thumb toward the door. "That hunka hunka burnin' love paid the check, overtipped me, and said he'd never had better food. And it wasn't until he was gone that I recognized his wife."

"H-his wife?" Meredith stammered.

"Yeah," she drawled. "Delia Pierson. She was my saving grace in high school. She did that YouTube series about self-affirmation, about being your own person, finding your own self, and keeping the faith when everyone around you falls apart."

"YouTube video series?" Meredith looked surprised, but Julia had dealt with youthful offenders and viral videos in her courtroom. "People do that?"

"Tons, and for every possible issue, but Delia's a Southern girl, and when they had that horrible bullying problem in the schools, she started speaking out and doing videos. They went viral, and schools had to start adjusting how they approached things. Some of them have even outlawed cell phones in the classroom."

"I would hope so," Julia muttered.

Meredith raised her phone as she stood. "On the plus side, let's go back to my place and see if we've got anything worth chasing. Unless you're too tired?"

"I'm hoping there's more of that flan."

"My thoughts exactly."

They moved toward the door as Jem Baldwin strode in. He stopped just inside the door, folded his arms, and faced the women. "You broke into my car and took my laptop. I want it back. And I want it back now."

Dodgeville, Wisconsin
September 1931

"Lawson." Hans lifted the baby boy and showed him to his mother. "That will be his name, named for his grandfather and great-grandfather, Lawson James."

Lawson?

Carrie struggled more upright. "Hans, no. We spoke of Matthew, remember? A strong, biblical name. Or John. David. Or Daniel, who defied a king. We picked those to choose from."

"But that was before I held him," he boasted, smiling at her, then into his son's face. "He is my father through and

through, and his father before him. Lawson it is, and he will be blessed by the example of many strong men."

"No." Was that her voice, so low? So commanding? So frightening when it was her who was frightened at the thought? "You cannot simply change a child's name without my blessing, Hans."

"And yet it's not a change, for we had not yet decided, my love," he exclaimed. Didn't he hear the anguish in her voice? Didn't he see the angst in her eyes at the very thought of giving this baby a name so close to the little boy lost?

"You brought him into this world with such courage and conviction and strength, Carrie." He knelt down next to the bed, but all she could sense was the forbidding expression of his mother's face behind him. "If you don't wish it, of course we can use another name. Matthew. That was a favorite of yours, wasn't it?"

It was. Her first choice, but when she looked up she saw her mother-in-law's stern features looking back at her. Not mean. But not one bit friendly, either. She took a deep breath. Was it worth bearing the wrath of a single-minded woman for the rest of her life?

Yes, if it meant not using a name that was so close, so very close to the lost child that peppered her dreams and captured her thoughts far too often. But when his mother folded her arms across her chest, awaiting the verdict, she gave in. This baby gazed up at her with the same accusatory look of the woman standing firm against the wall, so maybe that's

what God intended all along. That no matter where she went or what she did or how deeply hidden she remained, she would never forget Lawrence, a child swept into obscurity to hide the truth. And whatever truth that might have been, she'd become a partner to the masquerade, and she hated herself for that.

Chapter Ten

"YOU THINK WE STOLE YOUR laptop?" Julia hadn't spent over a decade grilling witnesses and lawyers for nothing. She folded her arms and met Jem Baldwin's stern look with one of her own. Only, in her opinion, better. Tougher. And she was quietly proud of that. "What is the matter with you? We haven't even left the restaurant."

"Before you got here. I stopped at the grocery to grab some soda, then came here to pick up my dinner. Your car was parked outside the grocery store when I went in. I got a phone call, and it took me a few minutes longer than expected. When I came out, your car was gone, and the two of you had moved your Girl Sleuth act over here."

"Be careful what you say," Julia warned him. "I don't take false accusations lightly, and we've never been near your car."

"You took pictures of it."

Meredith jumped in now. "Of course we did. We're running an investigation on similar people. It's only smart to know what to look for. And why would we want your laptop, anyway? First, I expect it's password protected."

His grimace confirmed her supposition.

"And second, what have you discovered that you need to keep secret? Or maybe a better question is, what are you looking for that's so volatile that anyone would chance stealing your information?"

"Don't answer a question with a question." This guy wasn't just irritated. He was downright angry. "Who'd have thought that two old Southern—"

"Old?" exclaimed Julia. She'd learned a long time ago that "old" was your age plus twenty years, so she had a long way to go, and no one—*no one at all*—ever got to call her old.

"You'd best get out of our way before I give you a good old-fashioned Southern purse whompin'," Meredith threatened. "Let's see who's old then, Jem Baldwin."

His jaw went a little lax, then he firmed it. "Why did you want the laptop? Why not just ask me for information?" He dropped his voice as Charlene moved their way.

"Is there a problem here, ladies? How can I help?" she asked in a tone that rolled with a thick molasses feel. "Mr. Baldwin, was your food satisfactory?"

He sighed. "It was wonderful. But there is a small matter of thievery."

"Not performed by us," Meredith cut in.

"The car—" he began again.

"Do you know the license plate number?" pressed Meredith.

He pinched the bridge of his nose, then sighed. "I do not. But it looked like yours. It was a silver SUV."

Julia persisted in their interrogation. "Why would you leave something so important in your car? Was the vehicle locked?"

"Of course it was."

"Broken into?" asked Meredith.

"Nothing was broken, but the back door was unlocked and the laptop case gone."

"Did you leave the back door unlocked? Sometimes our key fobs mess up."

"I'm not stupid," he shot back, and Julia leveled a look at him that said she wasn't quite so convinced. "All right, did I double-check and make sure the doors were locked on my car? No," he answered his own question. "But I double-clicked and my horn beeped, so of course they were. And if it wasn't you two who got into my car, then who was it?"

Meredith looked at Julia.

Julia looked back.

Then they both faced Jem Baldwin. "Well, that's exactly what we need to find out, isn't it?"

Chapter Eleven

JULIA'S PHONE RANG AT SIX fifteen the next morning. She jumped up, grabbed the phone, and hit ACCEPT, certain that something dreadful had happened to Beau, but it was Meredith's voice that rang across the miles. "How soon can you get here?"

"What?" By the time she'd gotten home and into bed, it was after eleven.

"How soon? We missed our note-comparing time last night after that standoff with Jem—"

"You got me out of bed to compare notes?"

"No." Meredith's voice dropped. "I remembered where I saw that photographer's sleeve, the one surrounding Lawrence's picture. Ron's sister Barb was doing a heritage album a few years back, and some of the Bellefontaine pictures had that sleeve. I remember she removed some of them to fit the album, but she photographed them all in their original condition. We need to drive up there and check it out, but they're leaving for Maine this afternoon, so we have to act fast."

The ringing phone had spurred a head rush, but the thought of being able to track down a concrete clue chased the threatening headache away. "How far is it? Ninety minutes?"

"Nearly two hours in weekday traffic," Meredith replied. "I thought if we leave by eight and get there by ten, we can be out of there with enough time to track down any leads we might get and not mess up Barb's time frame."

It was certainly worth a shot. "I'll be there. My makeup won't be stellar, and you know how I am about my makeup."

"While being one of the most naturally beautiful women to walk the planet." Meredith sighed loud and long on purpose, an old, standing joke. "Yep. I know."

Julia laughed. "See you by eight. Have coffee ready."

"In a to-go cup, with cream and sugar."

"Done." And when Julia arrived at 7:58, Meredith was true to her word. She hurried out the door and got into her car. Behind Meredith's house were just enough parking spaces for hers and one more car.

Julia parked her car and climbed into Meredith's SUV. "I'm still rankled that Jem Baldwin automatically put two and two together over his missing laptop," she admitted as Meredith pulled away from the curb opposite Pulaski Square. "But now he's got me curious about what's on the laptop. What is he hiding? Am I overreacting?"

"No, ma'am." Meredith headed toward the expressway as she spoke. "You are spot-on. So is he just a hardworking author who's understandably upset about a theft? Or is there something more going on that you and I aren't aware of?"

"That's the question, but what could it be? He's a well-known New Yorker, he's got great street creds, and he's here to round out a story. So it could be frustration and anger over being targeted."

"Wouldn't he save his notes and story in a cloud?" Meredith raised her eyebrow. "Don't we all?"

"Fear of plagiarism?"

Meredith frowned. "I think a writer would utilize any backup that's available, and I can't even imagine a program that doesn't have cloud backup resourcing today. Let's say that's a given, okay?"

Julia nodded.

"Then we have to assume that he's upset because someone might find something he doesn't want revealed."

"No writer wants a manuscript leaked," said Julia. "I've seen how quickly books get pirated these days, and it's ridiculous. And people who download them seem to have a casual disregard for the thievery aspects of the case. First it was music, now books. The stealing of intellectual property wasn't big in juvenile court, but it's there in the upper courts. Every time someone puts a lock in place, there's a hacker waiting to dismantle that lock."

"You're right." Meredith kept her eyes on the road as she cruised toward Charleston. "But there could be more to it. I can't prove it yet, but his reaction went right to being judge and jury and accusing us, and he seemed just as dumbfounded that it might not be us, which means that really surprised him. So was it coincidence or not? If he was deliberately targeted, that means we have someone else keeping an eye on Jem Baldwin and his research."

"A jealous author?" Julia mused. "Money? Stolen ideas? It's not unheard of for people to take others' ideas and run with them. Plagiarism isn't nearly as rare as people think it is. My friend Marta sees this kind of thing all the time." Marta Bourret had been one of her law school study partners at the University of Virginia. They were two of a group of six who provided a united front through the first two arduous years of law school. She and Marta had gone on to become judges, and Marta had been appointed to the state Superior Court two years after Julia accepted her juvenile court position.

"I've seen it in the news too," Meredith replied. "Songs that get lifted and redone in another genre. Although how they figure that out is beyond me when there are only so many notes."

Julia wasn't sure how they'd assess that either, but as she sipped the coffee Meredith had made, she sent a quick text to Carmen. CHECK OUT PLAGIARISM AND JEM BALDWIN, PLEASE. SEE IF THERE ARE ANY HITS.

WILL DO, came back the swift reply, and within five minutes, Carmen had texted her several links, all of which had Jem Baldwin's name and the word *plagiarism*, but as Julia read the articles aloud to Meredith, one thing became abundantly clear.

Jem Baldwin wasn't plagiarizing anyone, but the best-selling author's work had been targeted a number of times, and that would give anyone reason to be suspicious.

They pulled into Barb Metcalf's pristine fifty-five-and-over gated community just after ten, and Meredith's sister-in-law met them at the door. "I'm so glad you made it up here," she exclaimed as she pulled Meredith into a hug. "I have simply hated being so far away from you in your time of trial, Meredith, darling, but I know that your ardent faith and even stronger nature have stood by you in this storm."

Julia bit her tongue. Bit it hard.

A two-hour drive might not be the easiest thing for Ron's sister and her husband, David, but a phone call, text, or email wasn't all that difficult or time-consuming. Barb had done none of those things since Ron's death eighteen months before. Any contact had been instigated by Meredith, and bless her heart, she'd kept trying all the while, because she wanted her sons and her grandkids to feel like they were part of the Bellefontaine family. Barb's lack of communication wasn't much help. Fortunately, Ron's other sister, Gwyn, was just the opposite of Barb.

"Barb, this is my dear friend Julia Foley."

"Formerly a Waverly, I believe." Barb said it with a bright smile, but dredging up Julia's very middle-class family was like a quiet shot out of a loaded gun. "It's so nice to see you again, Ms. Foley."

"Judge Foley," Julia corrected her. "A pleasure, for sure."

"Now Barb, I don't want to keep you, I know that you and David are busy packing, but you had some of those old Bellefontaine pictures that you used in your online photo book, correct?"

"Dozens," Barb gushed as she swung the door quietly shut behind them. "Simply dozens, and it was such a chore to get those loaded in the proper manner, of course, but I was fortunate to have professional help."

She dragged out the word *professional* to show that she was not only smart enough to call in help as needed, but had the funds to do so. Julia bit back a frown and had to restrain herself from glancing at her watch. She did it. Barely.

"And it's a marvelous gift to the entire family," Meredith assured her. "Your generosity has not gone unnoticed."

"One never knows." Barb's expression faded slightly. "So many in today's generations fail the basic courtesies of thank-you notes, but I suppose it is what it is and there's no helping how one was raised."

Her words seemed to insinuate that Meredith's sons didn't bother sending thank-you notes.

Meredith didn't act one bit offended, but Julia was offended for her, so that evened things out. "You know, my boys are probably guilty as charged," Meredith told Barb, "and your brother wouldn't have sent a note of kindness or appreciation if I didn't write it for him and poke it beneath his nose for a signature, so I understand your frustration. And the two of you, raised by the very same parents," she added, laughing, but making her point in a most genteel way. "Who would ever think such a thing? We don't want to get in your way, so if you could show us the hard copies of those pictures you had scanned, we'll check out the photographer's name and be on our way."

"Surely you'll stay for lunch," Barb protested, but Meredith shook her head firmly. Julia almost hugged her.

"We would never impose like that when you're trying to get out the door. You have a long drive ahead of you, and I could not live with the guilt of delaying such a wonderful holiday. Are the pictures in Dave's office?"

"I wouldn't dare," Barb confessed in a low voice. "Even though he's been done working for four years, he is absolutely obsessive about his space. I've got them in these clever totes in the spare room closet, away from heat and light and what-all. Old photos are such a treasure, aren't they?"

"They truly are." Meredith followed Barb into the room. Julia followed Meredith, but she didn't hurry. She glanced around Barb's fairly sterile house, and a glimmer of sympathy hit her.

Barb and Dave had three kids. There were no pictures of them on the wall. No grandchildren photos except for a few on scattered table-tops. No cozy sayings brightened niches or nooks, the refrigerator bore no child's artwork, and when she crossed into the spare room, the floral comforter and pillows were the only sign of color. Everything else was off-white meeting a rug-covered light-toned hardwood floor, the same floor that went from room to room throughout.

"Here we are." Barb opened the bin of pictures and set it on the bed. "Which pictures are you looking for?"

"The ones in the cardboard sleeves," Meredith explained, "that had that little embellishment along the bottom. Not a fleur-de-lis but a scrollwork."

"Cardboard sleeves?" Barb's face puckered instantly. "Who would keep old pieces of cardboard? I'm sure I tossed all of those years ago."

"All of them?"

"Dave can't abide clutter, and I couldn't see keeping every little scrap of this, that, and the other thing. Was that what you were after? The sleeves?"

"The photographer's name, actually. In case he or she has archived historical shots."

"Oh, I have that," Barb assured her. "As part of our documentation I noted things like that in the hard copy version of the timeline." She opened a top drawer of a desk and withdrew a thick book. Then she perched on the edge of the bed and opened it. A table of contents took her quickly to the correct page and she ran her finger down a list of notes, then paused. "M. Ellis Linkletter, Linkletter Photographic Studios."

Julia jotted it down while Meredith peered over Barb's shoulder. "Is there a photo of the sleeve? Or a remnant of it anywhere? Just so I can be sure it's what I'm looking for?"

"Well, there is this redone photo that I had made because the original was absolutely fused to the cardboard, as if someone had glued it around the edges. We couldn't withdraw the picture without risking its integrity—"

Integrity of pictures? Like trimming that quarter-inch around the edge might mess up the world as they knew it? Once again Julia fought the urge to say something, because *if you can't say anything nice, don't say anything at all.*

"Ah, yes, here it is." She opened to a page and held the book out for Meredith's inspection. "That's the photo of Great-Great-Grandma Bellefontaine when she lived near Washington Square. While all the Squares of Savannah have their own unique charm, I find Washington Square to be the most appealing. Don't you?"

"I find them all quite lovely," Meredith replied. The fact that she had inherited her great-granddaddy's home as a newlywed had rankled Barb for a long time. "But I do love taking my coffee out onto the back deck and gazing at Troup Square. The military aspects remind me to be grateful for those who fought for my freedom."

"I suppose that's another way of looking at it," Barb said, frowning.

Meredith's response was a more intense focus on the task at hand. She bent low, examined the picture in the book, then raised a look of triumph to Julia. "It's the same scrollwork design."

A tiny rush raced along Julia's spine. "Really?"

"Exactly. And photographers liked to use their own personal designs on their sleeves. It made them recognizable. This appears to be Linkletter's choice."

"A logo that predated logos."

"Exactly." Meredith took a shot of the picture with her phone's camera then set the book aside. "Barb, thanks so much for letting us invade your space this morning. And thank you for your keen attention to detail. It's been a big help."

"Ron and I were a lot alike in that way," Barb replied.

Gaze down, Meredith hesitated.

Julia wasn't sure what she might say.

Ron had been a good man, but he sometimes had a heightened image of himself. Confident, and even a little cocky at times. He and Barb shared that trait, but Ron's strong work ethic and sense of humor had created a strong business, giving him reason to crow.

Meredith's hesitation only lasted a moment. "People of strong opinions," she replied, and she said it with a winning smile. "And a willingness to share them."

"Much like Mama."

"Indeed." Meredith slung her bag over her shoulder. "Barb, thank you. We'll get on with things and let you get back to your packing."

"I'm so glad you stopped in." Barb led them to the door. "And we'll be back midsummer, although that's a preposterous time to return, isn't it? I'd love it if you drove up for lunch sometime."

"Call me," Meredith replied. "And thank you again." They left, got into the car, and backed out of Barb's driveway. They'd made it halfway down the first street leading out of the secluded cul-de-sac when Meredith breathed out a sigh. "I am not sure whether to be insulted that she won't call or simply quietly satisfied that she won't call."

"Either works," said Julia cheerfully. "I'd go with a blend of both and be done with it. There's no changing Barb at this late date unless the good Lord does it Himself, and we have a very interesting lead to follow up on. I can't tell you how excited I am." She almost crowed the last words as she pulled out her phone and began typing *Linkletter Photography* into the search engine.

Chapter Twelve

"You know it's never that easy," Meredith warned Julia as she finished jotting notes onto her miniature pad of paper.

"Except this time it might be," Julia muttered. She put down her pen and scanned the links indicating that a Martin Linkletter in Mount Pleasant was hosting a show of his great-grandfather's work. She clicked for directions, and the GPS took over. "Are we going to stop and visit Carter or his family while we're so close?" she asked. Meredith's oldest son lived in Charleston.

"I called and told him I'd be up this way, but he was busy."

Too busy for his mother?

Just as Julia shook her head, Meredith's phone rang. She answered it with her Bluetooth. "Carter, hey."

"Mom, are you really coming up here today?"

"Already here," she told him.

"To visit Aunt Barb, you said?"

Meredith winced in Julia's direction. "Yes." She paused a moment, then went further. "Julia and I are looking into something of historical significance, and your aunt had a clue for us."

"You're on some sort of case?" Carter didn't try to mask the note of disapproval, and Julia was pretty sure he didn't realize that she could hear him.

"We are," Julia said brightly to clue him in. "Carter, this is fascinating work. After so many years of having people present me with evidence, I now get to hunt for it, and what a learning curve that is. Your mother is quite patient and positively brilliant. But then, of course, you know that."

His tone changed quickly. "She's amazing, all right. Well, would you ladies like to meet me for lunch in about two hours?"

Meredith glanced at the map read-out on her dashboard and nodded. "That would be perfect timing. Where would you like to meet?"

"Let's find somewhere that won't be too crowded," he suggested.

Meredith hesitated, but then he added, "I've got to get back to the office, so if we go someplace that's packed full, we won't have much time to enjoy the visit. How about I pick something up, and we meet in Waterfront Park? That way I don't mess with my three o'clock conference call."

"It sounds perfect. I'll text you when we finish up in Mount Pleasant, all right?"

"Yes, and Mom? Be careful. Please." He added the please almost habitually.

"Happy to oblige," she told him. "See you later."

She glanced at Julia as they approached the expressway entrance. "Suffice it to say he's still got serious reservations about this venture."

"For your safety? Or his convenience?" Julia wondered, and Meredith arched her right brow.

"Both, I'm sure. If I'm tucked away in a museum or doing tours for the historical society, I'm in my niche and he doesn't have to worry. What he doesn't understand is that with all of Ron's faults, he knew better than to try to compartmentalize me. He liked being larger than life, he liked being in charge, and that worked, because it was his company and clients really related to that take-charge persona. Letting that go didn't mean I wasn't willing to stand my ground when I needed to. It simply meant I was smart enough to pick my battles. So was he. I think in the end it kept our marriage strong, but I don't think Carter sees that. Not yet, anyway."

"I saw it, and when Ron would get a little too presumptive about something, you had a knack for reeling him in."

Meredith slid a glance her way and winked. "We all have that knack. Don't we, darling?" and the way she said it made Julia laugh.

"True words." The GPS interrupted with instructions for an upcoming turn, and in a quarter hour, they were on Martin Linkletter's street. They parked a few houses away and faced one another.

"You take lead," said Julia. "I'll be backup. If it goes south in a hurry, I'll ad lib something judicial."

They walked up a short driveway, past a late-model sedan, and knocked on the door. A man answered quickly. He opened the door, looked at them, and frowned. "I gave at the office?" He deadpanned the phrase, then added, "Really. I mean it. I do that community fundraising thing. And it's a school, not an office, but don't hold that against me. And I don't go to church, so if that's what you're after, I am a lost cause and a waste of time."

"No one's a waste of time or a lost cause," Meredith assured him as she adjusted her purse strap higher on her shoulder. "But that's not why we're here. We've come calling because your great-grandfather did some photography work in Savannah, and the internet linked your name and address to his former studio."

"You're history buffs?" Now his brows shifted up.

"She is." Julia indicated Meredith. "But we understand that you've got a love for history as well."

"I teach four high school classes every term, and I'm head of the Social Studies department. Every year I lobby to increase the focus on history, and every year I get voted down, but I refuse to stop trying."

"My kind of man," Meredith assured him. "We saw online that you've made a display of Ellis's work."

"I did, and we have it posted in my wife's art studio. You can't live in this part of South Carolina and not be acquainted with an art studio," he went on. "Not as prevalent as Cape Cod, but still impressive. Anyway, I did an overview of his work from 1915 to 1928. Once the Great Depression hit, his business folded, and by the time money became available again, he'd developed some kind of disorder that left him unable to handle the equipment, according to my grandfather. Parkinson's, maybe? No one really knows and it didn't get passed down. Would you like to go see the display?"

"Yes."

"We'd love it," Julia added, and within a minute he'd locked the house and was leading the way around Coleman Boulevard until he pulled off onto a side street, then into a parking lot. He waited for them, then indicated an old but renovated building on the southwest corner of the lot. "Rose's studio." He said it with true pride in his voice. "We met at the Cape when I was young and stupid but smart enough to realize she was amazing. And here we are, thirty-four years and three kids later." They fell into step beside him, and when they went into the studio, Julia was instantly struck with the calm beauty of the place. It oozed fanciful tranquility, and when a middle-aged woman approached them, she spotted Martin and smiled. "Ah, you good man! You've captured more, I see. Well done!"

"Why do I feel like I've just stepped into a fairy tale and we might become tonight's main course?" Meredith whispered to Julia. "Of course, these paintings set the tone, don't they?"

"Rosie, these gals came to see my exhibit, but I think your fairylands have captured their attention."

"Meredith Bellefontaine." Meredith held out her hand.

"And Julia Foley," said Julia, as she shook the woman's hand. "And this work is fascinating."

"Southern and ethereal," noted Meredith.

Rosie laughed. "It's amazing how much fun you can have by painting fairies and wee folk into streetscapes and landscapes. It draws people in. Except not this heat, so we're thrilled when people swing by this time of year. Customers are scarce in the heat of a Georgia summer."

"It's important to guard the bottom line, that's for sure," Martin added.

"It is oppressive outside, isn't it?" Meredith asked sympathetically. "In our favor, we do have the ability to 'glisten' down to a science, don't we?"

Julia had turned slightly. She spotted an array of old photos in the next room. "Is this the historic display?" she asked Martin.

"It is." He led the way into the room and Julia had to admit, he'd done a great job of arranging the pictures in not only a pleasing way but chronologically enough that they told a story of their own, right through the faddish dress codes of the roaring twenties, and then…

Nothing.

"It stops here and never goes on. He had two sons and a daughter, but no one else picked up a love for photography like Ellis did," he told them. "They sold all of his equipment when he died, and I'm just grateful that they boxed up all of this and his customer albums so we could get a glimpse of the early twentieth century through his lens."

There were many family shots, done in the somewhat stern style of the time. But there were impromptu shots too, of couples strolling arm in arm with heads close together, of picnicking families on blankets in the park, and young mothers out on a brisk walk with their babies tucked into prams.

"These are wonderful." Meredith smiled at her, then addressed Martin. "You said Ellis kept albums?"

"Yes, he did," Rose said. "In fact, he's been approached by a well-known producer who wants to use the Linkletter collection in a PBS documentary. They were impressed with his meticulous chronological albums that he kept of various families throughout the years."

"Was the Green family one of those?"

"He gave them a generous section, because not only did Sully and Patrice give of their time and money, they were very good to everyone, no matter who they were or what their background."

"We've heard that before," said Julia. "May we see the Green pages?"

Did he hesitate? Julia thought so, but then he crossed the room. "Of course. We don't touch this with our fingers, so you can either put on gloves"—he motioned to a box of disposable gloves nearby—"or use the eraser end of a pencil to turn the pages." He reached below a thick wooden counter and withdrew an album. He set it on the counter, slipped on a pair of the gloves, and opened the book carefully.

Several early pages of the thick volume were dedicated to the Green family. Ellis had even added newspaper clippings that featured them.

There were nearly twenty newspaper shots of the Green family, interspersed with their semiannual professional photos. First with a wedding shot of Sully and Patrice, and what a look of love they shared for that photographer's portfolio. Not the standard look-at-the-camera-and-smile pose, but a face-to-face look of undying affection between the handsome groom and his beautiful bride. Part of her hair was coiled into an updo, unusual for the time when simpler styles were becoming the rage, but the abundance of curls swept just past her shoulders. She looked like a princess, and his expression said that he knew he'd claimed a marvelous prize. "What a great shot."

"And he continued to catch the family with great shots, partially because Patrice liked to be very open about letting the children be themselves. Be children."

That was certainly true of the photo Harlowe had shared with them, and as Meredith carefully flipped the page to family photos, Julia hoped they'd stumble on one with the missing child in it. That wouldn't be too much to ask, would it?

"Their three children." Martin didn't try to mask the pride in his voice. "Ellis got them climbing trees, playing hide-and-seek, and riding horses. All three loved going to the parks to play. Harlowe wasn't the most photogenic of the three, although he was a good-looking child."

He was right.

While Bertha and Wilma smiled with youthful abandon, Harlowe's expressions were more subdued, and yet, in his earliest photos, he seemed just as joyful and carefree as his younger siblings. "May I take a couple of snapshots with my phone?" Meredith asked.

Martin shook his head. "I'm sorry, we can't risk harm to the pictures from flash photos."

"Even if I use no flash?" Meredith pressed.

He frowned. "No. I'm sorry, we have to have certain rules to maintain the integrity of the display."

"I understand." She let it go, but when they turned to the final page of the Green family, the first thing Julia noticed was the change in Patrice.

The happy, proud mother had disappeared.

She didn't appear abnormal, but the beautiful, loving smiles of the former pages were gone, and in their place was the look of a woman who'd known suffering.

Meredith pointed to the second-to-last page. "What year are these from?"

"1921," Martin told her. He took out a magnifying glass and held it over the base of the picture. "At some point my great-grandfather penciled in dates on some photos. These are all 1921 or later."

After Lawrence was gone.

After the child disappeared, a child who had no note or image in this photographer's carefully laid-out book.

How could that be? They knew he'd taken photos of Lawrence. They had a copy of one, so why wasn't he recorded in this book?

"Did Ellis include all of the Green photos in this book?" Julia asked, and she was careful to look straight into Martin's eyes this time.

He didn't hesitate. "I assume so. Nothing else has been found, and as you can see, the book has been carefully organized, year by year."

"Well, you've been a tremendous help," Meredith told him.

Had he?

Julia didn't think so, but she smiled and nodded politely. "Yes, thank you. Thank you both."

"Our pleasure, ladies." He walked them to the door. "Do you need me to get you back to the expressway for your trip home?"

"We're fine, but that is most chivalrous of you in a day when chivalry is in scant supply," Meredith assured him.

Julia didn't groan. Yet. While she wasn't used to being a novice on the job, she understood the benefit of Meredith's kindly and feminine ways when Martin's expression relaxed. "It was my pleasure, ladies," he repeated.

They walked out the door, smack-dab into the full force of Georgia heat and humidity. They hurried to the car. Meredith turned it on, blasted the AC, and exited the parking lot. When they were five minutes away, tucked on a small side road, out of sight, she parked and pulled out her phone. "I couldn't sit there and make notes in case he saw us, but I don't want to forget my impressions."

"Of?"

"Missing pictures." Meredith scribbled onto a small notepad she kept in her purse. "The pages were unevenly faded in spots, meaning someone had removed pictures that had been there and rearranged others to fill the spaces. And there were a few dots of old adhesive. I think there were at least five missing pictures. Maybe just four, but either way, someone removed photographs and shifted others."

"You could tell that?" Julia chalked up another line in the plus column for her friend.

"When one has pored over enough historical annals to fill a small museum twice, one sees the signs." She emphatically drawled the words to make her point. "And the distinct difference between Patrice's expression in 1920 and 1921 tells a story. But what is the story?"

Julia hadn't offered this idea up to this point, but after seeing those pictures and noticing the same thing, she had no choice. "What if she killed her child, Meredith?"

Meredith didn't look quite as horrified as Julia expected, nor all that surprised. "I can't deny I'm wondering the same thing," she said softly. "Something affected her in a tragic way. She's got the affect of a person suffering post-traumatic stress, and it's there for years, so it had to be something awful. Simply awful. And what could be worse than a child's death at your hands?"

Julia's heart sank. She'd seen years of heartache in some of the families dragged into her courtroom, and she'd witnessed the heavy hand of fate on some of them. How grief grabbed hold and hung on for way too long. And that sometimes people used that grief for other things.

"Do you think she was trying to replace that little boy with those later pregnancies? The ones that miscarried?"

Julia sighed. "I think that's an understandable reaction. And grievous too. Do you think Harlowe knows? If she did something that caused Lawrence's death, do you think he knows and he's buried it subconsciously, but he doesn't want Jem to stumble on it and reveal the family tragedy?"

Meredith bit her lip, then motioned to the clock. "I don't know, and we've got to get over to the park. But we stumbled onto something today, Julia. I'm not sure what, exactly, but I can promise you one thing. It wasn't one bit good."

Julia was 100 percent certain that her friend was right.

Chapter Thirteen

CARTER WAS TYPING SOMETHING INTO his phone as they approached, but he put it aside when he saw them and came their way. "Hey, Mom." He hugged Meredith, then smiled at Julia. "You're still in?"

"By my own volition," Julia assured him and laughed. "I can honestly say I'm learning a lot from your mother and feeling like a newbie. I haven't been a novice at anything for a long time, but who says you can't teach an old dog new tricks? I'm living proof that you can."

"But nothing dangerous, right?" Carter's gaze went from Julia to his mother. Then he sighed.

"Well, I can't guarantee the elements of human nature," Meredith said, "but we're not hunting down the FBI's Most Wanted, so we've got a degree of safety. And we are quite capable, Carter. You know that."

"It's not the capability," he told her as he led them back to a shaded picnic table. The breeze was warm, but it *was* a breeze, and it felt good beneath the shade of the tree. "Dad was licensed to carry, he was a certified sharpshooter back in the day, and just his size was enough to intimidate people. Not to mention his manner."

Meredith didn't discount his observations. "You're right," she agreed. "And that was beneficial in a lot of our cases, but then there were some that really profited from a different touch. And that's where I came into play. I know you tend to see history as obsolete, tucked neatly into a box of the past, but it's rarely that way. It often rears up and affects things happening today. So that's the niche we can fill. Julia's eye for evidence and culpability and my historical knowledge."

"Just so long as you're careful."

Julia was pretty sure he didn't mean to be pigheaded. It was actually kind of sweet how concerned he was. But his concern only spiked her desire for success.

"I'm a sharpshooter myself," she told him, just to see his reaction.

His mouth dropped open. "Aunt Julia, are you carrying?"

"A woman doesn't sit in judgment in a Georgia courtroom and not realize the need for self-defense," she answered frankly. "I've never once had the need to use it, nor do I expect to, but the need to have it was quite clear."

"Let's hope you can keep that record of nonuse." He stared at his mother for a few seconds, as if trying to reconcile himself to this new image, then waved to the table. "I had the deli pack us lunch."

"Carter, it's wonderful." Meredith smiled up at him and took a seat on the far side of the table. "This is so much more fun than trying to carry on a conversation in a crowded restaurant."

"Thanks, Mom." He looked almost relieved that she liked it.

"How are the kids handling soccer and baseball in this heat?" she asked as she opened her to-go container.

"Complaining but plugging through. They're both at camp for the next two weeks, at the lake and with a pool, so they'll have their swimming lessons, some diving time, and rowing."

"That's a wonderful experience for kids," noted Julia. "You're following in your mother's footsteps," she continued. "She always told me that she kept you two so busy you didn't have time to get into trouble."

"There's some truth in that," Carter admitted with a smile. "But I think it was mostly because neither one of us ever wanted to disappoint Mom or Dad. Dad because he was a larger-than-life character—"

"He loved you to distraction," Meredith cut in and rolled her eyes at the thought of Ron being intimidating.

"We knew that, but we were smart enough to respect the size factor too," Carter said as he picked up his sandwich. His phone rang. He took it out and silenced it without even scanning the caller, and that meant his mother was more important than work.

"What if that was Sherri Lynn?" asked Meredith.

"She's got her own ringtone," he told her. "And there is nothing so pressing that it can't wait thirty minutes, right?"

"Right." She smiled at him, obviously happy for the thirty-minute allotment. Julia knew the kids had busy schedules. Meredith had told her about the sports they played and the clubs they belonged to, but Sherri Lynn's mother had passed away six years before. Meredith was the only grandmother the kids had. She'd mentioned not seeing Kaden and Kinsley as much as she liked, but they made it a point to get together on a semiregular basis.

Chase made the trip to Savannah often. He was four hours away, but he'd come to Savannah on a Friday night and hang out until Sunday midday, then drive back. He did this at least once a month, and sometimes they'd just meet in the middle.

Two boys, now men, and to hear Meredith tell it, so different.

"How is work?" Meredith asked him. She tended to keep to safe subjects with Carter.

"Busy," he told her. "The presence of Hunter Army Airfield has spurred the growth of a lot of industry, including the aerospace industry." He took a gulp of his soda. "And its size lends itself to shoring up the economy, providing jobs for a lot of people."

"So if I was looking at investments in the loan market," Julia began, and Carter raised a hand.

"I can't speak to that, Aunt Julia. I'd hate myself if I gave you bad advice, and there are still some parts of the market that are vulnerable. If I steered you wrong, I'd never be able to forgive myself."

"I'll let you off the hook," she told him but then raised her sandwich. "But only because you picked a great combination for this sandwich."

"Mom's favorite."

Julia glanced at Meredith.

Italian blend subs and sandwiches weren't Meredith's favorite. They'd been Ron's favorite. Meredith liked fancy chicken salad with pecans or sliced real turkey with lettuce, mayo, and lots of salt and pepper on soft bread.

But then Meredith surprised her.

She leaned forward and held Carter's gaze. "I'm absolutely enjoying this, but chicken salad is my favorite. With nuts or without, I could live on chicken salad and die a happy woman."

Carter looked from her to the sandwich, then sat back slightly. "Dad's favorite, right?"

Meredith nodded and took a bite for emphasis. "And don't get me wrong," she said once she'd swallowed. "I'm thoroughly enjoying the lunch and the company, but it's always good to set the record straight."

He pulled out his phone and tapped on the screen. "Chicken salad, with pecans," he said as he tucked the phone away. "Now if I mess up, I've got backup to keep me solid."

"You didn't mess up, Carter." Meredith put a hand on his arm and squeezed lightly. "A sandwich is just a sandwich, after all. But time with you is a wonderful thing, and I appreciate you taking time from your busy day to have lunch with us."

A tiny chime sounded just then. Carter's phone, likely a reminder that lunch was over.

"Glad it worked out," he told her as he stood. He leaned over and gave her a kiss on the cheek and a hug. "Duty calls. I've got just enough time to get back to the office, meet with some folks, then handle that three o'clock call. Thanks for meeting me here."

"Loved it," she assured him.

"See you soon, Aunt Julia. And keep her out of trouble, okay?"

Julia smiled brightly. "No promises, but I'll do what I can. Unless I'm the one getting us into trouble, that is."

He gave her a slightly strained smile before he turned and hurried toward the nearby parking lot. He wasn't twenty steps away before he withdrew his phone and made or answered a call, right back in full business mode, but that was all right. He'd prioritized time with his mother, and that was all that mattered.

"He wrote it down." Meredith lifted her water bottle, took a generous swig, then set it down. "I can tell you each boy's favorite food, movie, television show from various years, teachers, and milestones, but my son had to write down that I like chicken salad."

"He is a man," Julia reminded her. "And I'd be more affronted about that if my very own husband didn't have to do the same thing on a regular basis."

"For real?"

Julia laughed. "Yes, ma'am. And it's not a problem with aging, Beau has been somewhat obtuse to those things from the beginning. He's always had his head wrapped around the newest techniques in medicine and anesthesiology, so he can give you a breakdown on significant progress from clincial trials dot gov, but he wouldn't be able to tell you what my favorite coffee beverage is. The fact that Carter cared enough to write it down says a lot about his character. And about how he loves you."

Meredith smiled. "You're a great friend, Julia."

"I try. But I'm not saying one thing that isn't 100 percent truthful. Men may not always be the most observant creatures in the world. Ron was the exception because that was the nature of his job and he did it well, but if you asked most men to cite the details of their significant other's likes and dislikes, I expect most would fail miserably."

"Then I'm glad he made note of it." Meredith's phone buzzed. She pulled it out, scanned the display, and gasped. "Harlowe's just been taken to the hospital in an ambulance. No word on his condition, but it was lights and sirens all the way."

"Oh no." Julia didn't know the old-timer like Meredith did, but she wasn't about to let him go to his eternal reward without some sort of resolution on this case. No man should have to face the Lord with something grievous on his soul. "Let's get back there, quick. But Meredith," she began as they raced for Meredith's car, "what if it's fear that's put him in this condition? Fear that we might find out the truth? What if his mother didn't kill that little boy? What if *Harlowe* did, and she hid the truth? That kind of guilt would wreak havoc with her head, wouldn't it?" She climbed into the car.

"Oh my word, Julia, it would, and how would you sacrifice one child, especially a small child like Harlowe would have been at the time, when you've already lost a child? A mother's instinct is to shield and protect."

"But what a burden to carry." Julia might not have children of her own, but the thought of a twofold tragedy wasn't unknown in courtrooms. How one tragic moment often spurred others.

"Oh, it would be awful. Do we dare ask Harlowe about it now? If he's fighting for his life?"

Julia tapped her hand along the passenger side door, then faced Meredith more fully. "Do we dare not? Because if he needs God's forgiveness, I'd rather he get it on this side of the heavenly gates than deal with it when he gets there. That doesn't sound one bit appealing. Does it?"

"You're right, of course." Meredith merged into the fast lanes with finesse. "When I was a child, I spoke as a child," she paraphrased softly. "And if that old soul has carried a burden like that all these years, I want it lifted before it anchors him any further."

Julia clasped her hands and offered a silent prayer that they would be in time, but more than that—

That they would find the answers that plagued an old man's soul.

"I do not understand a mother like this," Lorah Engstrom hissed. "A beautiful child, nearly five years old, and she barely looks his way. It is as if I am raising the child myself, Hans, and that is not as it should be. You should do something about it."

She hissed, yes, but made sure it was loud enough for Carrie to hear, yet it was nothing she hadn't heard before. Nothing she'd done for the child was right in the older woman's eyes. Nothing she said was humble enough for the strict woman's ways, and when she chose not to fight back, to avoid the quarrelsome words and intimidating tone, things didn't improve.

They grew worse until her sweet-natured son was more the senior woman's child than hers, but maybe that's what the scolding woman had wanted all along.

Pretending oblivion, Carrie kept weeding a row of thick-leafed pie plant, ready to be stewed for canning. She'd learned much since coming north. Lessons she could take with her, if it came to that.

Hans crouched down beside her. Behind them, his mother scolded Lawson for picking flowers, and Carrie's heart ached at the sound. Didn't all children love to pick flowers?

"We should go away," Hans said softly, and for the first time in years, her heart leaped like it did when he courted her.

"*To a place of our own,*" she replied quickly. "*A place where it's just us. You. Me. Our child. A place where I can raise him my way. Our way.*"

Surprise lifted his brows. "*I meant a picnic, nothing more, love. A day away to revitalize all of us. The first crops are in, and my father can do the milking for a day. Would you like that, Carrie? A day away?*"

"*But then we would come back, Hans.*" She sat in the fine Wisconsin soil and faced him. "*And it would be as it always is. I say something. Your mother disagrees. And you take her side. You side with her about our house, about this land, and about our child. He's more their child than ours now, isn't he?*"

He started to argue, but she raised a hand for quiet. "*You see it. You know it. But you will not or cannot face her and take my side. She owns this land. You want this land, so you won't cross her, but that leaves me on the outside. Always outside, looking in.*"

"*My mother is strong, not evil. Her mother was strong. Her sisters too.*"

"*So I am weak?*"

Distress drew his brows together. "*You have a sensitive heart. That is not a weakness. But it has an effect, I believe.*"

An effect.

Her heart plummeted.

Sorrow gripped the very core of her being.

He thought her weak. He wouldn't use the word, but it was there in his face and his carefully chosen speech. He'd allowed his mother to step into Carrie's rightful place so often of late. Making decisions about their little house, their garden, and the most important thing of all, her little boy. But as she saw Lawson place his hands on his little hips, in a move much like the older woman's, reality dawned.

Carrie had no place here. Not now. Maybe she never had and had simply fooled herself into thinking Hans loved her just the way she was. He did, back then, but her different ways stood between him and his parents and the land he'd helped tame for nearly thirty-five years. The choice loomed crystal clear now. He would never choose her over the land. And she couldn't stay and watch her beautiful child become a caricature of his harsh grandmother.

Her heart wept, but she kept her face serene. If Hans knew her plan, he'd stop her. Not because he longed for her to stay, but because it would be the right thing to do, and what a sad commentary on their short marriage that would be.

She'd make her plans and slip away during the frenzy of harvest, when no one had time to come searching. She'd go off on her own and begin anew. She'd done it before. She could do it again.

Chapter Fourteen

"FALSE ALARM." DELIA SPOTTED MEREDITH and Julia coming through the door leading from the hospital's parking garage and hurried their way. "But what a day it's been!"

"What happened?" Meredith asked. "Is he all right?"

"They're still doing tests, but I think he's fine. He was having a regularly scheduled scan done to make sure he's still cancer free, and he complained that his chest hurt."

"His heart is fairly old," noted Julia, and Delia didn't disagree.

"And yet quite fit," she told them. "It turns out the strap they used to hold him still was too snug for his comfort, and it wasn't his heart. He was just cinched in too tight."

"So he's fine?"

"Yes, but how nice of you both to come right over. To worry about him. He is blessed to have friends like you." Then Delia looked more carefully at Julia. "Except you still look worried, which means something else is bothering you. Can I help you with it?"

Julia grimaced. "I don't think so. Not without your uncle's permission." She exchanged a look with Meredith and then sighed. "I think we need to ask him, Delia, because I'd actually appreciate your input on all this. Harlowe trusts you, right?"

She nodded. "Absolutely."

"Then we'll see if we can bring you in on the conversation. We were just discussing concerns for his health and the book and our investigation when we got the call, and neither of us want to see Harlowe gone before we get some answers."

"Those must be mighty serious questions." Delia pressed her lips together, then nodded. "But I've always respected Uncle's privacy and zest for life, so I'll bide my time. But today's scare made me realize that we might not have much time left."

She was right.

Meredith drew her purse up onto her shoulder and said, "We'll come see him tomorrow. After he's had a chance to rest and recover from today's activity. I'll call Myla and set up a time."

"I can meet you there," Delia offered. "He'll have a harder time saying no if I'm there. He really does love me."

Meredith accepted the offer quickly. "Then yes, meet us there. I think a little coercion is just what the doctor ordered."

Julia texted Myla when they got back to the car, and Myla set them up for a nine o'clock appointment the next morning. She texted Delia, and when a thumbs-up emoji came back, she settled back into her seat and sighed. "I think the adrenaline rush is ebbing. I was so worried that we might lose Harlowe without some kind of confession. Or at least an honest exchange. If he or his mother was responsible for the loss of his little brother, then that's way too much weight for a kindly old gentleman like him to carry."

"Agreed." Meredith turned onto Macon Street and parked in her spot beside Julia's car. They were just getting out of the car when Jem Baldwin cruised to a stop behind them, blocking Julia's car in.

He parked the car, jumped out, and came their way, looking absolutely frazzled. Was it the research? The heat? Humidity?

All three, Julia decided when the flush on his cheeks deepened.

"May I help you, Mr. Baldwin?" The chill in Meredith's voice would have kept ice cream cold on a mid-August Savannah sidewalk.

"Tay Tay Pomeroy. Is she working with the two of you?" He wiped a clutch of tissues over his forehead, then the back of his neck, and the tissues left tiny shreds of paper in their wake.

"Cotton works better," Meredith told him. "Washable, absorbent, and friendly to the planet."

Julia frowned. "I have no idea who Tay Tay is or what you're talking about."

"I know Taylor. Tay Tay," Meredith added. "She works at the salon I go to. She's also a real history buff. She's a frustrated writer and has a real knack for doing big hair. Really big hair." She frowned at Jem. "But how did you come in contact with her?"

"I'm talking with folks who have worked for or with the Green family. The Pomeroys have done both. I needed a trim, so I made an appointment with her for this afternoon. Can we talk inside?" He mopped his forehead again.

Meredith hesitated, then said, "Of course. But you'll have to park on East Charlton and come through the front door." She turned to walk through her gate then unlocked the back door. She and Julia entered the house and went up the back stairs to the main floor of the house. "I'll let Carmen know we're here," she said to Julia. "You can go let our visitor in."

Julia opened the front door and waited for Jem to climb the stairs. She waved him in and guided him to the formal living room.

"Have a seat," she said. He pressed the damp tissues to the back of his neck again, and she added, "The cool air will help."

"I avoid Manhattan heat and humidity in the summer by going up to the Adirondacks," he explained. "But I didn't dare wait with this research, considering Harlowe's age. And Tay Tay Pomeroy was willing to share some interesting facts and allegations about Sully and Patrice that need confirmation, but I don't feel right asking Harlowe about his father's affair. If, indeed, there was one. I'm not putting a lot of stock in Ms. Pomeroy's veracity."

Meredith had just reached the door when he uttered the last couple of sentences. Her eyebrows shot up. Her mouth opened. But before he could turn to acknowledge her presence, she'd composed herself and moved forward with ice waters. "Tay Tay has a bona fide love for history, and she's willing to share all she knows." To Julia she added, "Mamie's Super Cuts is a few blocks north. Tay has a chair there. She's quite reasonable and has an illustrious clientele. The irony is that you'll never hear a peep out of her about her current clients. She's amazingly tight-lipped, but when it comes to history, Tay is a fount of knowledge with no OFF switch."

"She's a talker. But here's my dilemma," he continued, and as he cooled down, he looked less combative. "She's giving me tidbits of things that are undiscoverable. I can research old business dealings. I can uncover shady contracts and investments, but when it comes to the human element, I have to tread lightly."

"As most should, and in today's social media frenzy, those words are quite refreshing," Meredith told him. "I've never heard a word that impugned the Greens' marriage or their relationship, and I headed up the historical society for years. It seems to me if there had been trouble in their marriage, someone would have noted it. They may not have had social media access, but the ladies of Savannah knew how to gossip. And because Patrice kept herself away from that kind of thing, she became the target for even more gossip."

"How so?"

"Some called her aloof. Snooty."

"Most likely she was just an introvert," Julia said.

"Exactly." Meredith sipped her water as she sank into a chair. "Good buttered biscuits, that heat and humidity have drained me, and I'm used to it," she told Jem. "This isn't exactly the season for northerners, is it?"

"I will take your advice, buy cotton hankies, and keep to shade and AC," he replied. "So you know nothing about this Netta Wilson person?"

Meredith almost dropped her glass. She recovered quickly, but it was clear that the name startled her. "Other than historical context as a long-standing family in the Savannah community, no." Her reaction said more than her words.

"And yet the name surprised you," Jem said.

Julia couldn't argue that, so she hoped Meredith had a good explanation.

"It did," she admitted. "My husband's family was quite well acquainted with the Wilsons. They were neighbors and friends in earlier generations, and even intermarried, so we're shirttail relations on the Bellefontaine side. My surprise was in hearing them connected with the Greens, because the Wilsons didn't bother to hide their extreme jealousy of the Greens, who weren't hit as hard by the Depression as most everyone around them. The two families didn't share opinions on much of anything as far as I know. In fact, the Wilsons were caustic to just about everybody, and hard to get along with. I think your research will back me up on that."

He studied her. "I understand what you're driving at. Those were hard times, and suspicions and rumors ran rampant. I can see you both understand the need to present things honestly while not deliberately hurting others."

"The fact that we're talking eight decades back, more or less, thins the veil, though," Julia offered. "We all know that things were different then. People reacted to circumstances in ways they would never have in normal times."

"Agreed. And because of that, I'm going to tread carefully," he told them. He stood and set his glass down. "Nothing I've found about the Greens implies that they gained their fortune illegally or that they cheated anyone or hoarded their money. Quite the contrary. They were financially supportive of white and black business-men in this community, and Sully was one of the first in the area to provide annual scholarship awards to black high school seniors. But sometimes even the most generous acts can't stop vicious rumors, if you know what I mean."

Sadly, Julia did after years of courtroom experience. "I wish I could disagree with you, but I can't," she told him. "But I also appre-ciate that you won't jump to any conclusions that cast a pall on Harlowe's family."

"I assure you, I won't," he told them. Then he turned toward Meredith. "Thank you for the cool air and the water. The heat was getting to me."

She rose and showed him to the door. "My pleasure. And thank you for your attention to detail. That's something I've always appreciated in your stories. Now I see that it stems from careful research."

"You're welcome." She opened the door. He stepped through it, and he'd no more than descended the half-dozen steps when Meredith blew out a breath, closed the door, and collapsed into a chair. "Julia. Oh, Julia."

"What is it?" Julia kept her voice low just in case he'd stopped to listen, but when his car engine started, Meredith replied.

"Netta Wilson. How could I have forgotten that little detail that might not be so little after all?"

"You think he's right?"

"I think Netta Wilson was a miscreant who played havoc with several marriages in the Roaring Twenties. Let's just say that propriety took a dive and loose morals had their day. We have to research this, and I feel terrible that it took Tay Tay Pomeroy to remind me that there were other factors at work back then. Factors that may have played a role in this mystery. Even though I never heard a whisper about Netta and Harlowe's father, there were several other implications. She was considered the femme fatale of her time."

Her words disappointed Julia. She realized then that she'd gotten to know Sully and Patrice through the investigation, and liked them. Wanted to solve their problems. But if Sully had an affair with a nefarious woman, that voided a lot of her sympathy. "Shall we go see this Tay Tay character?"

"Oh, the way you say that is so funny. It is a silly name, isn't it? And yet it fits her to a T. I'll call and find out when she's done working."

Carmen came into the room. "You two have had a day of it, and I'm starved, and the diner has fried catfish and dirty rice as a special. I've got some things to go over with you, but first a question. The guy that was here just now? He's the author who's doing research?" She reached for her purse.

Meredith grabbed her bag too. "I'm not dinner hungry because we had a late lunch, but coconut custard pie will win my heart. And yes, that was him. Why?"

"I went up to the library to chat with Rebecca about something a few hours ago."

"He's been doing some research there."

"Except he wasn't in the library." She frowned. "He was in the park, watching everyone who went by. Not obviously, but when you've lived on the streets, you never lose your awareness for things out of place. And he was out of place, pretending to read a newspaper in this heat. In the park. When there are perfectly good restaurants or air-conditioned places close by."

"Maybe just trying to get a feel for the area," Julia suggested.

"He'd want to do that so he can portray Savannah accurately, I expect," agreed Meredith.

"All well and good, but when Maggie Lu came strolling up for her shift, looking so pert and lovely in that trim gray dress with the white collar, all of a sudden he perked up. Got a couple of shots of her with his phone, then texted someone. So what does this rich guy want with Maggie Lu? Hasn't she already been scrutinized enough?"

"Why would he care about Maggie Lu?" Meredith frowned.

Julia shook her head. "Does she have a relationship with the Greens?"

"Not to my knowledge. Would he be researching the Besset family for his story?"

"Maybe his story is going deeper than he's letting on. They are sagas," noted Julia.

"Well, it looked funny," Carmen declared, "and I don't intend to see any high-and-mighty Yankee author pester a woman who's done nothing more than offer the best she has to teach children."

Carmen's rough teen years had shaped her into a streetwise woman with a big heart. "Your protective side is showing." Julia smiled.

"Hmm." Carmen frowned as she made sure the door locked behind them. "It held me in good stead for a bunch of years. Mostly," she admitted grudgingly. "I suppose there were a few scrapes I should have avoided."

"You think?" Julia exchanged a grin with her. "And yet here we are. Doing just fine. And Beau comes home tomorrow, so my ladies' nights are going to be interrupted until he leaves for that Canadian fishing trip next week."

"I love that he's enjoying his retirement," said Meredith. There was no lament in her voice. "That's how it should be, but we're wise enough and faithful enough to know that God's the great time-keeper. He numbers our days. And even though I don't share Beau's penchant for fishing, I'm amazingly happy that it freed you up for our joint efforts. Having the two of you on board has turned a spark of a dream into reality, and I can't thank you enough. But now I want to find out what Baldwin's game is and what Maggie Lu has to do with it. Immersing himself in the flavor of a community is fine.

Bothering Savannah's women is not, and I am going to make sure that doesn't happen."

"Except—" said Julia. "This is the age of cell phones, ladies, and after living in two major cities for all these years, I've seen folks take pictures of absolutely anything and everything. It's different now," she reminded them. "There's no cost involved. And maybe authors use the pictures for inspiration."

"You do make a valid point," Meredith replied. "And he did come to us for our take on Tay Tay's information. That was pretty stand-up of him, wasn't it?"

"It was."

Meredith slid into the driver's seat as Carmen took a seat in the back. "I'll keep an open mind," she promised Julia as she pulled away from the curb. "But when there's an easy opening, we'll delve. And we'll see what Jem has to say. Or, more importantly"—she made a right turn and glanced Julia's way—"what he doesn't say. Because that could tell us a whole lot more."

Chapter Fifteen

"OH MY WORD, WHAT'S GOING on here?" Meredith slowed the car to a crawl as they approached the intersection just south of the diner. "Look at that line."

"Are they all waiting to get in?" Carmen asked. "Are they giving food away, and I missed the memo?"

Julia clapped a hand to her head. "Triple J's post to social media. Remember how Delia sent it right out?"

"With a 'best burger I've ever had' tagline," Meredith recalled. "Do you think that's what's caused this?"

"The power of social media," Carmen said. "Triple J has over three million followers."

Meredith's mouth dropped open. So did Julia's.

"They're from all over the country, but a huge chunk of them are here in Georgia. Ladies, I give you the results of social media in action." Carmen pointed out the long, winding line of people stretching down the tree-shaded sidewalk with a wave of her hand.

"There's no way Charlene was ready for this," said Julia. She scrambled out of the car as soon as Meredith found a parking space a few blocks up the road. "We've got to help her."

"Help her? How?" asked Meredith.

"We'll let her guide us," Julia replied as they hurried up the street. They took a left turn to go to the back door of the busy diner. Julia rapped on the door sharply then opened it. The mouthwatering scent of fried fish mingled with grilled meat, and at that moment it didn't matter that she'd eaten a hoagie three hours before. That food smelled good! "Charlene, how can we help?" she called across the kitchen. "What can we do?"

Charlene turned, spotted her, and threw her three aprons. "Bus tables. Dishes. I've got Savannah Food Supply on its way with more burgers, cheese, and coleslaw mix, and the bakery is bringing twelve dozen rolls right over. Everyone is ordering burgers and sweet potato fries. I've never seen anything like it."

Julia distributed the aprons, and the three women got to work.

"Either of you know how to run a commercial dishwasher?" Carmen asked. "Because I do."

"No, but we know how to carry dishes," Julia replied. "We'll bus. You wash. We've got this."

For the next three hours the women worked nonstop, and when the diner drew near to closing time, the line finally ebbed. Then stopped.

And all three of them took a breath, the first one they'd shared since coming through the kitchen door.

"I can't even imagine how many dishes we've toted and washed," Meredith drawled as she and Julia carried the last two full totes into the kitchen. "In forty years of marriage and raising two kids, I haven't come close to doing something like this." She burst out laughing and shoved a shock of her blond hair back behind her ear. "I liked it!"

"Land o'mercy, that was a workout. Check your wrist, what's your step count?" Julia asked as she deposited her last tub of dishes onto the stainless steel counter.

"Thirteen thousand seventeen!" Meredith beamed. "A new record. That means I can have my pie with a clear conscience."

Julia hated to mess with the hopeful look on her friend's face, but facts were facts. "The pie case is empty."

"No." Meredith stared at Julia, hurried around front to the glass-fronted dessert case, and looked like she was about to burst into tears. "It is empty. Ridiculously empty."

Tara was scrubbing down the counter area and refilling the salt and pepper shakers. She slipped around Meredith, crossed through the kitchen, and came back with two brand-new pies. "Coconut custard and pecan," she told them. "They delivered new ones this afternoon, but it was too busy for me to even think of getting them out here and properly cut."

"And that pie is on the house," Charlene told them firmly. "Ladies, I'd have never gotten through this without you, I can't even imagine how this all happened, but then someone told me a football player put a picture of his burger out on Instagram and everybody went all crazy and came down here, and we might be declared the Best Savannah Diner by *Georgia Trails* magazine. All of this is just about too much for a fairly new owner like me to take in, but I'll take it." She grinned and hugged each lady in turn, including Tara. "Yes, ma'am, I surely will. And my poor mama couldn't get near the place to grab supper tonight, so I told her I'd drop food off for her, but she said no worries. She'd have soup and crackers at home, because nine thirty is far too late to be eating a meal. Packs the pounds on, you know."

"She's slim as a reed, so she's got something going right, for certain," Carmen replied.

Was this a good time to tell Charlene about Jem taking pictures of her mother? Julia hesitated, but Meredith waded in. "Hey, Carmen noticed something today, over by the library. The author who's in town, researching a story—"

"Baldwin. He's ordered a few meals here," Charlene said.

"Yes. Well, it seems he snapped a few pictures of your mother this afternoon and then texted someone. Carmen saw him and thought it odd."

"It is absolutely odd. Who would want pictures of Mama walking to the library? And what would his interest be in her?"

"Well, she's a well-informed Savannah resident who has seen the good and the bad of history. Maybe he wants to interview Savannah residents to get their take on things," said Julia. "I would think he'd need that to get an accurate picture of life here, don't you?"

"Then I would expect he'd ask questions first and snap photos later," Charlene replied in a no-nonsense voice. "Mama is just settling into a routine after dealing with the whole Besset Plantation dustup, and that was the past creepin' up on the heels of the present, wasn't it?"

"And yet that worked out well in the end," noted Carmen, and her words seemed to calm Charlene down.

"It did, and Mama is actually better off now. And at peace, and that's something we couldn't have said before. So you don't think I should go off half-cocked about this, I take it?"

Carmen shrugged. "I think we'd be smarter to figure a few things out first. If we discover he's up to no good, we handle it like the Southern ladies we are."

"Purse-whompin'!" Meredith declared, although Julia was certain she'd never given anyone a purse-whompin' in her life. The thought of her ladylike friend brandishing her petite designer purse as a weapon was enough to make her smile.

"I vote for pie and a fresh start tomorrow. All in favor?"

"Aye!"

"And me too," said Tara as she finished wiping down the farthest tables. Then she frowned and bent forward. When she stood, she held an envelope in one hand and a picture in the other, and not just any picture. Tara raised the very same picture Meredith had in her purse, of Lawrence Green. Only Meredith's purse was safely tucked in the kitchen and had come nowhere near the dining area all night, so how on earth did this hidden picture show up in the crevice of a booth?

Julia had no idea. And when Tara read the words on the back of the nearly hundred-year-old photo, a cold thrust of fear shot right up her back.

"'Stop looking now. Or else.'"

The chill hit Julia's neck, raising tiny hairs in protest, but when she looked at Meredith, Meredith didn't look scared. Or even all that troubled. In fact, she looked somewhat triumphant as she whirled back toward Julia, and her words explained why. "Clearly we're on the right track," she said firmly. "Now we just have to figure out which track that is."

Julia didn't do threats well, but seeing Meredith's face and hearing her tone had an unexpected calming effect. What had she thought, getting into a business of investigations? That everyone on the planet wanted to be checked out? Looked into?

"Tara, may I have that?" Meredith asked.

"Yes." Tara handed it over, but her brows shot up when Meredith handled the picture with a white napkin. "Is this like evidence?"

"One never knows," Meredith told her cheerfully, and then she moved to the table and picked up a fork. "Pie first. Mystery-solving later." She tucked the photo into her purse's side pocket and sat down to have pie, and if Meredith could take this in stride, so could Julia.

The only question now was which pie to have.

Dodgeville, Wisconsin
September 1936

The September frenzy provided the opening Carrie needed. Everyone was working long hours between milking the herd, birthing new calves, the final cutting of hay to prepare for a long, cold Wisconsin winter, and the three cash crops Hans's father had insisted on growing. When Hans had tried to explain the loss of money due to the Great Depression that had settled on the nation and the world, his father had stuffed his hands in his pockets and said "Bah!"

And so they planted wheat, corn, and alfalfa for market, but beating the onslaught of cold, wet weather took time and effort.

She packed her bags quietly, taking nothing more than what she'd come with, and when she parked the wagon at the depot, she left a note affixed to the front seat.

Hans would find the note. He'd read it and be sad, but he wouldn't come after her. She understood that. She accepted it. But it pained every ounce of her soul to know that once again she wasn't special enough or worthy enough to be protected and beloved.

He would raise Lawson his way. Their way, she acknowledged, thinking of his straightlaced parents. He'd lament the breakup of his marriage, but he was far too busy to do anything about it, and in the end, he'd move on. Divorce her quietly. And live his life.

She stepped onto the train heading east. Vermont was noted for making cheese. A job there, a quiet life, penitent and solitary. If that was all there could be, so be it, but as the train engine chugged to life, her heart cried out.

She sprang up, ready to jump off the train and run back. Back to the wagon, back to the growing farm, back to the arms of the one man who'd tried to love her, but a bulky passenger blocked her way, and by the time the man had stowed his bag, the train had accelerated and her chance was gone. Just like that.

She could get off at the first stop and head back, but that would mean another ticket, and how would she explain her absence of hours? Would she even get back before they found the parked horse and wagon? And then she'd face the barrage of questions for which she had no answers, and so, when the train rumbled to a halt at the first stop, she folded her hands and stayed in her seat.

She'd made her decision with great thought. She'd follow it through the same way.

Chapter Sixteen

"WHERE DID THAT PICTURE COME from?" Julia whispered as they walked toward the car a half hour later. "And how did you keep your cool so well? I'm pretty sure my face was an open book of astonishment."

"Practice, I guess, but my heart about dropped to my knees when Tara held it up. Who was in that seat tonight? And how did they get their hands on the picture we have? Did they steal it from the copies I made? And why was it tucked into the seat like that? I was bussing that area," Meredith continued as they climbed into the car. "But there was no one I recognized there all night."

"How did they know we'd be there?" Julia could hardly breathe around this next thought, because it drummed up all the bad thoughts she'd had to deal with as a juvenile court judge. "Do you think someone was following us today?"

Carmen cleared her throat. "Clearly someone wanted you to find it. Which means they recognized you guys, but you didn't recognize them. So someone else is in on this game."

"Doesn't feel like a game from where I'm sitting," Julia muttered. "I was at the other end of the restaurant, where Tara was serving. Justine and Rhonda were taking care of the counter customers and that section. We'll have to ask them who was in that booth."

"That will narrow it down to about thirty people over the course of the evening," Meredith noted. "Thirty absolute unknowns. Does Charlene have cameras?"

Julia frowned. "I have no idea. Why would a restaurant have cameras?"

Meredith wiggled her eyebrows. "Oh, darlin', there's a lot of not-so-good stuff that goes down over a great meal, and cameras have a way of recording those things for the police. But I know money's been tight for her, so the thought of dishing out a lot of money for a camera system might have been way down the list. In any case, we should see her before lunch tomorrow. If this was any indication, Charlene is not going to have to worry about the success of her restaurant for a long time to come. Amazing how one single post can have such a ripple effect."

A ripple effect.

Gossip.

Netta Wilson.

A missing child.

A possible affair.

Puzzle pieces spun around Julia's mind. When she got home, Beau was waiting to greet her with open arms. He enveloped her in a hug that felt so good, she didn't want it to end.

When she reluctantly pulled away, he said, "You look done in, sugar."

"Well, I've been in the trenches with Meredith and I'm not sure what we've gotten ourselves into, but it did include the first threat to my being as a private investigator."

"Someone threatened you?" Beau drew himself up to his full height and slung an arm around her shoulders. "Not for real, right?"

"It sounds real enough," she told him. He led her over to the couch, and they sat together. It felt wonderful to have him home. To have him to talk to. She explained the case to him. He listened carefully. Beau wasn't a big talker, but he was a great listener, and when she was done, he laid his cheek against her hair. "I can't say I like this, Julie-bean."

He'd given her the affectionate moniker way back when they'd been dating. She'd loved it then and loved it now.

"You didn't like courtroom threats either, darling."

"I take threats against my wife seriously, that's a fact. So is this person trying to scare you off? Or does he or she mean business?"

"That's the question, isn't it? But this does seem to let Jem Baldwin off the hook, since he wasn't in the restaurant tonight."

"And of course a rich *New York Times* best-selling author couldn't slip money to plant a photo." He snuggled her a little tighter against his shoulder to make his point.

She slapped his leg lightly. "Hush, you. I was ready to exonerate him, but now he's right back on the list. We're running over to see someone named Tay Tay Pomeroy tomorrow. Do a little history probing with her. I have to say that trying to figure out a century-old mystery is a lot like sifting through the facts and fiction presented in courtroom arguments. It's hard to sort through it all."

"And yet you excelled at it."

"Thank you." She yawned. "When do you catch your flight for the Canadian fishing trip?"

"Monday morning, six thirty sharp."

She turned and gave him a kiss. "Five days of having you home and then a week gone, but I'll enjoy these five days," she said.

He laughed and kissed the top of her head. "Me too, Julie-bean. Me too."

***

"Thwarted by norovirus," grumbled Meredith the following Monday. Their scheduled meeting with Tay Tay had been postponed when half the staff of Mamie's came down with the gut-clenching illness. "But she's all better, and we can see her later. Did Beau get off okay?"

"He did," Julia replied as she laid out miniature pages of notebook paper on the solid maple table edging Meredith's gorgeous kitchen. "When he tried to explain how small the plane is that flies them into these hidden Canadian lakes, I put my hands over my ears and refused to listen. The words *skimming treetops* painted a vivid picture for me. But then, Beauregard Foley had some concerns over our threatening message, so we evened the score. And how could we have spent five days examining things and come up with nothing new?" she lamented.

"Well, it's all nearly a century old," said Carmen. "But one of Justine's regular customers said something odd to her."

"Such as?"

Carmen leaned in to add impact to her revelation. "That he'd be eating free for the next couple of weeks."

Meredith frowned. "I don't get it."

"It seems he had a secret benefactor who paid him to leave an envelope in a seat. 'Like an old mystery show,' he told her," Carmen reported.

"Seriously? When did she hear this?"

"Late yesterday when the old-timer came in all giggly. She said he even ordered dessert, and he can't afford dessert, so she knew she was onto something big."

Oh, the poor old fellow. "Does she know his name?"

"Papa Alvarez. That's what folks call him. No one knows where he lives, but Justine thinks he's been on the downside of life for quite a while. She said he's mentioned the 'camp' before, so she thinks he might be living in the homeless camp over by President Street."

"We can try an internet search," Julia said, "but if he's homeless we'll most likely tap out."

"I asked Justine to text me when he comes in again. She says he's there two or three times a week and that Charlene slips him big portions and packs his leftovers with extra things."

"When I was hungry, you gave me something to eat." Meredith paraphrased the beautiful scripture from Matthew's Gospel.

"If you two are off sleuthing when she calls, I'll text you, but if you're too far away, do you want me to step in?"

When Meredith hesitated, Carmen took a firm step back. "No worries, I'll just text you and you can come running."

There was an awkward silence. Then the phone rang.

Carmen went back to the kitchen area and the laptop she used there.

Meredith answered the landline that almost no one called anymore. "Bellefontaine residence."

Julia saw Meredith roll her eyes. Who in the world was it? She got her answer when Meredith switched to SPEAKER and she heard Beatrice Enterline, the woman who replaced Meredith as the head of the Savannah Historical Society, in midsentence.

"...saying that I'm *far* too entrenched in rules and meeting etiquette, which, of course, stems from your more laissez faire attitude, but I don't want to have an uprising. I'd be so very grateful if you could come to today's meeting and simply show me how you managed to keep order without a soul knowing you were doing it."

"Come to today's meeting?" She winked at Julia. "Julia and I are working, but we'd love to stop by."

"Except we don't have outsiders come in to a planned meeting any longer," Beatrice explained. "I've readopted the old policy of invitation-only membership. It thins the ranks but sharpens the sword, if you know what I mean."

"I have absolutely no idea what you mean," Meredith retorted. "By doing that, you keep out all kinds of good people who share your love of history. Why would you want that when it's hard enough to get younger folks involved already?"

Beatrice must have recognized the indignation in Meredith's voice. "And that is such a good point, a matter I'll happily discuss with the membership. Of course, if Julia were to become a member, we'd welcome a woman of her regard with open arms."

Julia shook her head. "No," she mouthed to Meredith. That was just simply never going to happen. Not while Beatrice was the head of that group. And why in the world was Meredith practically head over heels about going to one of the controlling woman's meetings?

Meredith made a face and kept her voice even with effort. "We'll be there at two, Beatrice. Both of us."

"And miss luncheon?" The very thought of bypassing the elaborate luncheon seemed to shock Beatrice.

"Our loss, of course, but duty calls, and working women must pick and choose carefully."

"Then we'll see you at two, and I won't do a thing until you get there. Although I will save you each a dessert."

"Gratefully accepted." Meredith hung up the phone and sighed. "Oh my word, she is as regimented as can be, but she does love and know her history. But not letting folks in?" She made a sad face at Julia. "On the upside, Tay Tay will more than likely be there, and two of the long-standing members are members of the Wilson family."

Now Julia understood Meredith's eagerness to attend the meeting. She thought for a moment. "Do you think it would be helpful to do some preliminary research on Netta Wilson?"

"Yes. And actually, Maggie Lu might have some insider information about the Wilson family. Her grandma was sewing for a whole lot of people from that neighborhood during the Depression. Maybe she shared a story or two."

***

"The Wilsons?" Maggie Lu's tone shifted up when Julia asked the question a half hour later. "Granny Luv stayed clear of the Wilsons for a number of reasons. Their harshness was well known, she told me, but when the Great Depression hit she sewed for anyone who needed anything. She worked for the Bessets during the day and did home sewing at night. Our house was tiny, smaller than most apartments these days, but Granny used to scrub and polish and say we were blessed to have three good rooms, and she was right. So eventually she had to take care of Netta and her mother and aunt, and she said it was a hard process."

"Hard because?" Meredith led the conversation gently.

A shadow chased the normal brightness from Maggie Lu's eyes. "The Wilson women didn't feel the need to respect Granny's prices, low as they were," Maggie Lu told them. "They would give her what they wanted, and Granny didn't dare complain even though it was pennies compared to what it should have been. The Wilsons had a reputation for finding flaws with people's work and refusing to pay full price for their services after the fact." She folded her hands in her lap. "But Granny Luv always said that hard times can harden you or they can sculpt you into a better version of yourself." She gave them a rueful smile.

"Granny said that Cherise Wilson was a high and mighty woman and that her daughter, Marianetta, was worse. Folks called her Netta and she had a roving eye, Granny said. There wasn't a man or a marriage that was considered safe from her charms, and that could include the Greens, who traveled in that circle."

"Were they friends, do you suppose?" Julia asked. It didn't seem like the Greens would welcome a family like that.

"Well, now, Granny had a saying about that. She was a smart woman despite her lack of formal education. She'd say 'The rich hang with the rich. The poor hang with the poor. Doesn't make them friends, but it's how things are done,'" she quoted.

Meredith probed again. "Did Granny say anything more about Netta?"

Maggie Lu frowned. She hesitated then shrugged. "I suppose it was all so long ago that it's no sin to pass the word on now. She said that one of her jobs was to let Netta's dresses out. She had put on weight, and they needed more room, but Granny was no one's fool.

She told me that Netta was with child, and that a month later she went off to visit a relative for a spell."

"This was before she was married?"

"During the first World War, so yes. And it wasn't something that ever got known forthright," she continued. "Folks may have talked, but no one knew for sure what went on. Granny said my mama was needing to be watched then." She paused and thought for a moment. "Mama was thirty-five when I was born, so maybe seven or eight then? Bigger, but needing care, of course. That would make it 1917 or so, wouldn't it?"

1917 or so.

The same time frame that Harlowe had given them. Only it wasn't Patrice having a baby.

It was Netta Wilson.

Chapter Seventeen

JULIA NODDED. SHE DIDN'T DARE look at Meredith. The timing was too suspect. Did Sully and Netta have a relationship? And did they have a child together? Was the mysterious Lawrence that child?

"That was a time of secrets," Maggie Lu reminded them. "More was said in looks than words, Granny used to say. But a bad look was sometimes enough to make horrible things happen, so she taught me to keep my chin up and eyes down. Enough to keep me safe till times got better. Which they have," she finished. She gazed around the recently remodeled library fondly. "It's good to see improvements happening all around, for all folks. That's how a country should be, I expect."

"I concur." Julia wasn't a big hugger, but she reached out and hugged Maggie Lu lightly. "That's exactly how it should be. And with Charlene's business getting so busy, are you able to get over there to get meals, Maggie Lu? Because if you can't, we can always bring food by. We'd be happy to do it."

"All that business is a blessing, isn't it?" The thought wiped the shadows of the past from her eyes. "Charlene is beside herself grateful to you two."

"We did nothing," Meredith protested.

"Oh, my girl told me otherwise," Maggie scolded, smiling. "You could have met that young couple anywhere you wanted, and you chose the diner, and look what a difference that one decision made. If that's not a Holy Spirit moment, I don't know what is."

"His guidance and Charlene's great food. A wonderful pairing," Julia said.

"And you ladies know that if I can ever be of service, I'm available. Life's too short to pass things off, important things, that is. It takes folks helping folks to make some things right."

Julia met Meredith's gaze, then dropped her eyes to Meredith's bag. Meredith nodded, then withdrew the copy of Harlowe's picture.

"This is why we're probing for answers," she said softly as she handed the photograph to Maggie Lu.

"What a beautiful child," breathed Maggie Lu. She studied the little boy and sighed. "Now this is a very old picture," she said after a moment. "We have these kinds of pictures in the early-twentieth-century exhibits. What can you possibly find out about this precious boy? Who is he?"

"Patrice and Sully Green's son," said Julia.

"You mean this is Harlowe?" Maggie Lu asked.

"No," said Julia, watching for Maggie Lu's response. "This is Harlowe's little brother."

Maggie Lu's eyes shot to hers. "Harlowe didn't have a brother," she said. "He had two little sisters, but no brother."

"Harlowe says he did. That he had a brother who disappeared when he was about four years old and Harlowe was five. Never heard of or spoken of again. He said it was as if everyone just wiped the slate clean and pretended he'd never existed."

"Never existed." Maggie Lu stared at the picture with such a look of rare sorrow that Julia felt it to her core. "Oh sweet mercy, there is such perfect beauty in this face. Isn't there?" she asked the younger women. "And that face tells its own story. Indeed it does."

Julia was about to ask what that story was when her phone buzzed a text. Meredith's phone buzzed at the same time. When they looked down, it was a message from Justine, saying that Papa Alvarez had been sighted at the diner.

MEET US THERE, Julia texted swiftly. LET'S SEE WHAT HE HAS TO SAY.

It took a moment for Justine's text to come back to them. ARE YOU SURE?

Julia typed, YES. WE'LL MEET YOU THERE IN TEN. She put her phone away and stood. "Maggie Lu, thank you for talking to us. I know some of the old thoughts and memories aren't something you necessarily care to bring up."

"If we don't speak of them, we doom ourselves to making the very same mistakes, don't we? And we've come too far to let that happen."

Meredith gave her a swift hug, waved to Rebecca, and she and Julia hurried to Julia's car. Four minutes later they were parked two blocks from the diner. The thick muggy air didn't hold an ounce of freshness in it. It smelled of city fumes and river plants, and when they drew close to another long line at the diner, the thought of an air-conditioned booth evaporated. They slipped around the back.

Charlene waved them in. "Justine said she texted you?" When Julia nodded, she waved them through. "She's in her usual station."

"On it." Julia led the way through the connecting door into the jam-packed restaurant. When Justine saw them, she pointed to a lone man sitting in a booth. A plate of barbecue and hush puppies sat in front of the old-timer. He eyed the fresh plate of food with such appreciation that Julia felt guilty for taking so much for granted. Her life was generously blessed, while this old fellow knew a very different existence.

She and Meredith paused by his booth. He looked startled, then suspicious.

Meredith bent low. "That looks amazing."

He tugged the plate slightly closer to his side of the table.

"We wanted to stop by and ask you a couple of questions about the other night."

He frowned.

"The night we found an envelope in a booth. This envelope," she told him. She pulled out an envelope that looked exactly like the one he'd slipped into the seat the week before.

His eyes rounded.

All of a sudden the joy at his meal, his appreciation, disappeared. He half stood as if ready to bolt, but Julia was in his way on one side, and Meredith was across the table from him. "*No Ingles,*" he told them in a thick Hispanic accent. "*No hablo Ingles.*"

And yet he could come into the restaurant and order?

Julia was about to question his words when a soft, bright Latina voice indicated that Carmen had arrived. Justine must have texted her also. "*Hablo Español,*" she said to the old man. She went on in a stream of Spanish that Julia had no hope of keeping up with, despite five years of Spanish in junior high and high school. Meredith looked just as blank. And when Carmen nodded, shrugged, and indicated the envelope with another lengthy discourse, they said nothing. They barely moved. If Carmen could get information out of Señor Alvarez without making him ditch his lunch, they would both be grateful. He listened.

Looked down…

Then he gave them a frightened glance.

Carmen leaned closer and seemed to reassure him about something.

Finally the old man sighed and said something to her. When he raised his hand as if to measure something, Julia realized he was describing something.

Or someone.

A minute later, Carmen nodded. "*Muchas gracias, señor.*" She slipped a folded bill into his hand quietly. "*Vaya con Dios, Papa.*"

He gripped the bill tightly. "*De nada, señorita.*"

She stood, backed away, and moved toward the door. When the three of them got outside, she put a finger to her lips. "My car's over here." She walked toward her aged Toyota, and they all climbed in. "The air doesn't work, but I wanted you to hear what he had to say before you go to your meeting. He said the envelope came from a woman, not old, not young, and medium. Not pretty."

"A plain woman?"

Carmen made a face. "He said not pretty, and medium, and there's not a lot you can take from that except plain and medium-sized? Anyway, he was outside the diner, watching the back door because Charlene puts food out there at the end of the day, but with it so busy that day, there was no food. And this woman asked him to go inside and leave the envelope in a booth. Just that. And she slipped him a hundred-dollar bill to do it. So he stood in line to go in with everyone else."

"A hundred dollars must seem like a fortune to someone in his circumstances."

"And I expect he speaks English quite well," Carmen told them. "So the person who bribed him to leave the envelope didn't necessarily have to know Spanish to communicate with him."

"So it was a woman." Meredith and Julia exchanged looks. Then Meredith turned toward Carmen. "You did great. Amazing, Carmen. And I don't want you to get the wrong idea about my hesitation this morning."

"Listen, Meredith, I—"

"It's the licensing," Meredith continued. "You can't practice without being approved, or we could all lose our licenses and the business. It's state law. I want you to know that being in the office and handling things is a huge part of the success of any business. I hope you never feel marginalized or left out. Unless for some reason we have to leave you out, and that is sometimes the case."

Carmen breathed a soft sigh. "Thanks for letting me know. I didn't want to overstep my boundaries."

"Honey, you're not just working for us, you're working *with* us," Julia assured her. "The only boundaries you have are those you set for yourself."

Carmen smiled at Julia. "You've been a good friend to me for these last ten years. I don't know what I'd do without you, Julia. Or how I can repay you."

"Keep baking," Julia teased. "You have no idea how happy that makes us. Both of us," she added, including Meredith in her look. "Even if it means that Mere has to walk a few thousand extra steps. Totally worth it."

"That comes from the naturally thin woman who has never had to count calories in her life," noted Meredith dryly. "Even so, I can't deny that your prowess in the kitchen makes me happy too. I'm going to miss it when the office reopens in a few weeks. Until we get the agency kitchen remodeled. Then you can go to town." She grinned and reached for the door handle. "Carmen, thank you. Now if you could help us with this next assignment—"

"A bunch of rich women talking history?" Carmen's dubious expression underscored her words. "Not a language I can speak, ladies."

"Which is exactly why we make a great team." Julia patted her hand. "And if you were to try that lemon cheesecake recipe you found, I'd be happy to tell you what I think of it."

"Something about lemon and heat just works, doesn't it?" She smiled at the women as they got out of her sweltering car. "My goal is to have enough money to afford a better car next year. A car with AC. Reason enough to tuck some away, right?"

They waved to her as she drove off while they walked the block and a half to Julia's car. "Let's give her a Christmas bonus that helps her toward that goal," Julia said. "It must be her youth that leaves her looking so fresh and good in this heat, in a car with no air-conditioning, but good gracious, that was a bake oven. Agreed?"

Meredith slung her seat belt into place as Julia hit the air button. "One hundred percent."

No jobs.

None.

Carrie felt stupid, for hadn't Hans tried to explain this very thing to his father and George had shrugged him off as a know-nothing?

She'd heard of it, of course. She'd seen the papers, although no paper was brought to the Engstrom farm. When she got to Vermont, she'd tried to hire on as a creamery worker, but no one needed help. Not her help, anyway. Big, strong men, men who were providing for families, got first pick for jobs, and by the time she realized the extent of the economic decline, she was almost out of funds and homeless. Where could she go? What could she do?

And then a window of opportunity cracked open.

"You're looking for work, miss?"

She turned quickly. A man stood there, holding his hat in his hands like a gentleman would. She gazed up into the kindest set of blue eyes she'd ever seen. "I am."

"I've got four children," he told her. "Not much pay, but I've got a farm to run and their mother passed on when the youngest was born. Do you know much about children?"

"I was a nanny for several years," she told him, and hoped he wouldn't ask for credentials that didn't exist.

"And you like children?" he pressed. His manner suggested he truly loved his children. Of course, he was literally grabbing a perfect stranger off the street to care for them, and that shouldn't be how it was done. Ever. *"I need help through November. After that is winter, and it's quiet and I won't have money to pay, but if you'd like a job for the time being, I'd be happy to give it a try. My goal is to not have the youngest burn anything down while the older one is daydreaming about wishing on a star or flying to the moon."*

"A dreamer."

"Ayuh. She's that, all right, and like her mama, but a body's got to have dreams, doesn't it?"

How did this middle-aged farmer understand what so many did not? *"They do. Where is your farm, sir?"*

"Willis," he told her, and he stuck out a hand. *"Willis Blodgett, and our farm is part of the lot that runs the creamery. I heard you were looking for work through that, and thought I'd see if I could catch you. And your name, miss?"*

"Caroline." She left off the telltale *a* on the end purposely. But should she give him her maiden name or her married name? Married, she decided. If Hans came looking, it wouldn't be with police. Sully and Patrice wouldn't be nearly so understanding. *"Caroline Engstrom. And you've caught me at a time where my choices run thin, as do yours, so I would like to give this a try."*

He motioned to the small but well-swept wagon. *"I'm ready to head out. Do you need a hand up?"*

She shook her head. *"No, but thank you."*

He reached for her bag as she did, and his hand closed over hers. He didn't jerk back but leveled a calm look at her. "A little bit of help's all right, isn't it, miss?"

"It is, and thank you, Mr. Blodgett."

"Willis is good. Keeps it simple, Miss Caroline. We're simple folk here, for the most part."

She'd known affluent people, common folk, a tough factory boss, and the stern boundaries of the Engstrom farm. Simple sounded fine. Just fine. "I like simple things, Willis. They soothe the soul. What are the children's names?"

"Hannah, Clara, Charles, and Lia."

"Beautiful names," she told him. He didn't quite smile, but an air of quiet satisfaction softened his jaw.

"It took some talk for agreeing, and my wife was not one to be swayed when it came to names her children would bear for life. 'Willis,' she'd say to me, 'You know I love you, and your name is fine, but this is a new generation, and our children are headed for a new time, and their names will take them there. So forget the old family names and let's use ones that will take them forward, not backward. I want names that no one in the family has used before.' And so that's how they came to be," he explained, "although I think there was a Clara way back, but when Jane presented it to me I kept my mouth shut, because neither one of us was about to go looking. And sometimes that's best, ain't it?" he asked.

He faced her as they hit a tree-shaded straightaway, heading into some of the prettiest wooded country she'd ever seen. "Don't look too far back, so we can move forward. It's what this place and this country's all about, I reckon."

"Even with a depression that's ruined everything?" She didn't mean to sound dramatic, but her life was one big drama right now.

"Hard times and good times, they come and they go. Get too giddy about one and too down about the other, life's a rough ride. So I look at them and work through both. Things work out, miss. They always do."

A sensible way of looking at things. Not blowing them out of proportion. Not settling when things went wrong, but plodding through.

She liked that.

Would the children accept her?

She didn't know, but she'd learned a good deal about cooking and baking on the farm, and she'd learned even more about tending children while in Savannah, so maybe—

Just maybe—

This could work out.

Chapter Eighteen

"NETTA WILSON HAD A THING for Sully Green."

They'd finally gotten a chance to talk with Tay Tay after a poorly run meeting. Beatrice had been interrupted and called to one side so many times that both women felt sorry for her. Meredith promised to touch base with her the next day, but right now, Tay Tay commanded all their attention in a corner of the sumptuous hotel lobby adjacent to the lavish dining room where the meeting was held.

"How can we know that?" Meredith asked. "It was so long ago. I've heard that she made the rounds of several marriages, but I've never seen anything amiss in the Greens' history."

"It's right in front of your eyes if you know where to look," Tay Tay replied in a matter-of-fact voice. "The photos of the time. Family pictures. Published pictures. In the early ones, Netta was a frequent visitor and if you pay attention, she's got her eye on Sully, big time. She managed to be near him in several, especially once he was engaged to Patrice and even after they were married. And then, like a door closing, she's gone. She wasn't listed at any more family functions. Not in any more Green family pictures or even in photos of events they were associated with. There's almost no mention of her. It's not in the documented words of the times, but it's there, in plain sight. In the pictures."

"Do you think the attraction was two-sided?"

Tay Tay frowned. "No way of knowing that, is there? Cheating can be done surreptitiously, and back then, many men were given a pass because it was other men writing the stories. But if it was suspected, it wasn't talked about in any of the historical diaries, whereas other illicit relationships were. So maybe he resisted her charms. Maybe the widely held belief that he was totally in love with Patrice was true, but Patrice ducked in and out of pictures a lot herself, so it's hard to know. I think Patrice was a delicate flower in a lot of ways, but then she also did a lot of good, especially as she grew older, and that's in her favor."

"Did Netta ever marry?"

"She did," Tay Tay confirmed. "In her late twenties. I think it was arranged, but maybe she just casually fell in love with a very rich man who was seventeen years her senior." Tay Tay's skeptical expression seemed to doubt the validity of that. "They never had children, and he often said it was a huge regret for him, that they were never able to have children together, because he longed for an heir, but it was impossible."

Julia looked at Meredith.

Meredith met her gaze and frowned.

"You obviously know about the baby." Tay Tay dropped her voice to a whisper.

"How do you know this?" Meredith whispered, although why they were so careful about a hundred-year-old pregnancy was a mystery to Julia.

"Her aunt's granddaughter wrote a memoir called *Daughters of the South* about forty years ago, and she mentioned that her cousin came to stay in their caretaker's cottage for a while. A retreat, they called it, but the author's mother said that it was clear she was expecting, even though she didn't venture out of the small yard surrounding the house. She said that one night she heard a loud wailing and angst, and then, eventually, the sound of a baby crying. But then she heard a motorcar drive off in the early dawn hours. A day later, Netta was gone and no one spoke another thing about it, but she heard the maids whispering in the garden one day. They said having that little boy must have been awfully hard on the mama to have to burn that much bedding."

A boy.

Julia didn't dare glance at Meredith. She knew her expression would say too much. "Did she signify a date in the memoir?" she asked.

Tay Tay thought a moment. "She did, but I read this years ago. The war had just ended. Men were flocking home, and so many people had died from the flu, that the author indicated it was easy to hide the un-hideable because of all the comings and goings. And so much sorrow. That would make it 1917 or 1918, right?"

An out-of-wedlock baby boy born to a woman who openly flirted with Sully Green. Had Sully arranged for the baby boy to come to his home? Be raised as his own, as if she were Patrice's child? And did that pressure eventually wear Patrice down? If so, what happened to the child on that fateful trip north?

Julia didn't like jigsaw puzzles. They frazzled her patience, but this was a living, breathing puzzle of people, places, and choices. What happened back then? And why did someone want them to stop hunting for the truth?

"Tay Tay, you're amazing," Meredith told her. "I knew you'd be a fount of information. I am so grateful."

"Well, with this whole book nonsense going on, I think we Southerners have to stick together, don't we? When that author came begging for information, I may have steered him up a bum tree or two. Some of those Yankees don't understand the South, and I wasn't about to give him anything good."

"But he *is* a great author," said Julia.

Tay Tay's expression smacked of doubt. "He's a rich author and a New Yorker, two reasons to lift my brows and make him find his own answers. And maybe waste some of his time," she added. "Let me remind you that while the Civil War was over a long time ago, the Yankees beat our beloved Atlanta Braves in the 1996 World Series. I was in County Stadium, cheering our boys of summer on. It was the last game ever played there, only to watch them lose to those New Yorkers, and I can't say I've gotten over it yet. Football's all right for some, but I love my baseball. Although a share of football's cheer-leaders take to big hair and that's my forte, isn't it?"

"No one does it better," Meredith assured her. "And I need to touch up my color next week. Do you have an opening, Tay?"

Tay Tay pulled up a calendar on her phone. "I've got a four o'clock next Friday open. Will that work?"

When Meredith nodded assent, Tay Tay tapped the appoint-ment into her calendar, then stood. "I must be getting back, I've got a four and five o'clock for highlights and they're identical twins. I'll see you next week, all right?"

"Fine." Meredith gave her a thumbs-up. "And thank you again."

Tay Tay paused a moment, eyeing Julia. "You know, I can make back-to-back appointments for you two next week, if you'd like. There's a layered blond that would go great with your skin tone," she told Julia, and she wasn't being snarky. "We could do it gradually so folks would barely notice. By October, you'd be blond again."

Julia loved the dignity of her gray hair. She looked in the mirror every morning believing that the natural tones supported an appearance of wisdom, but for just a second the thought of going blond sounded possible.

And then she pictured Beau's reaction and shook her head. "That's a kind offer, but I'll pass."

"Food for thought," Tay Tay told her, before she turned and hurried out the door.

"Blond?" Julia turned toward Meredith and reached up to her hair. "Seriously? As if I'm not drop-dead gorgeous enough?"

Meredith burst out laughing. "Oh, she has no idea how you feel about your stunning hair, and you held back nicely. Well done. Now, let's race home and look at those pictures again. If there's truth to Tay Tay's summation—"

"And some corroboration—"

"Then maybe we've discovered why Lawrence appeared in the family, then disappeared."

"Which doesn't tell us what happened," noted Julia.

"But knowing why may lead to us knowing what happened," Meredith said as they walked up the road to Julia's car. "Being forced to raise your beloved's love child could put any woman over the top, and since we have no record of Patrice having another baby boy—"

"And a double reporting of Netta having a baby boy at the right time—"

"Then we may have just solved a major part of the mystery," Meredith said. "This doesn't give us answers, but it gives us motive."

"And behind every crime lies some kind of motive." Julia's heart hung heavy at the thought. "But what does it mean, Mere? What did Patrice Green do to that little boy? And no wonder Harlowe wants answers before Jem Baldwin stumbles onto this. And even though Tay Tay may have steered him offtrack because of her love for baseball, he's smart and experienced. If it's to be found out in something as simple as that memoir, he'll find it. Which means we have to find the answers first."

She said it simply enough, but Julia honestly had no idea how they'd do it. A crime that old, that far removed, didn't leave much of a trail.

"Hansel and Gretel found their way home by following crumbs," Meredith assured her. "I know crumbs aren't very nourishing, but if we track them long enough and hard enough, they lead to bread. And in this case, those pictures might hold more clues than we gave them credit for. Let's see if Carmen's available to stay late. We can order Chinese food and see what we can find."

Because they'd skipped the ostentatious luncheon, the food and the task both sounded good. "I'll text Carmen," Julia said. "You order food. I'm in."

Chapter Nineteen

WHEN THEY STUDIED THE PICTURES again, they found exactly what Tay Tay had said they'd find, Netta with the family prior to the war and even during the war, and then she was gone. But what did it mean?

Julia understood the weight and weakness of circumstantial evidence, and so far they hadn't found one real piece that tied anything together. Was that normal? She had no idea.

Carmen and Meredith had put together a puzzle wall by the time Julia arrived the next morning. The cat sauntered by as she came into the kitchen, flicked his tail in disdain, and leaped onto a window seat to watch the world pass by.

When Julia walked in with a sack of breakfast sandwiches from the diner, she faced the wall of notes with a firm nod. "This is a huge help to me."

Carmen unwrapped the bacon, egg, and cheese sandwiches and put them on a plate. "Visual context?"

"Exactly," Julia confirmed. "When it's all spinning in my head I can't see it clearly, but laid out like this, like a crime show on TV, it starts to gel."

Meredith pointed to the distinct sections. "What we know," she said, indicating a timeline. "And what we think we know," she added, pointing off to the side. "I thought the chronology would help."

"It does," Julia assured her. She paused as she checked a text, then frowned.

"Are you all right?" asked Meredith.

"Fine." The text was from her mother. "Mom wants me to come by for supper. Wyatt's coming over, and it seems my absentee sister is low on cash in California and hitting Mom and Wyatt up for money."

"Oh, Julia, I'm sorry." Meredith and Carmen were both aware of the sour family dynamics surrounding Julia's younger sister. Cassie had been busy "finding herself" for decades, generally at other people's expense.

"Me too," added Carmen. "If ever sisters were polar opposites, it's got to be you two."

"I haven't seen Cassie in twenty years," noted Meredith. "Not since she walked away from that precious boy."

"Most days I'm glad she did," Julia admitted. "Wyatt's such a good man. My mom and dad did a great job raising him, and he thinks of Mom as his mother. He was only nine when Cassie took off. And then losing Dad in that horrible accident was hard on all of us. To have Cassie breeze into town for the funeral then right back out again, all at Mom's expense, was rough." Her forehead tightened like it always did where Cassie was concerned. "I was so mad at her. When we were thinking about children and then couldn't have them, Beau and I used to marvel at how careless Cassie was with her precious son. In the end, she did him a favor. But what a weird family dynamic it makes."

"Weird or normal is often weighed in the perspective," Meredith reminded her. "Every family has a story. It's how we handle those stories that makes a difference, and your family has handled this brilliantly. Wyatt's a successful forensic auditor, your mother is amazing, and you've been wonderfully successful at helping hundreds of people while rendering smart decisions. We can't change the Cassies of the world, but we can take the goods God gives us and do our best with them. You and your mother have certainly done that with Wyatt. And his two little girls couldn't possibly be cuter, could they?"

"Madison and Kennedy call me Nana now," Julia admitted. "I love it. Mom is Grandma, and I'm Nana, and it feels good. But the tone of my mother's text means that Cassie is rattling cages, so I'll head over there tonight and see what's up."

"That storm's supposed to roll ashore sometime this afternoon," Carmen reminded them. "Not a hurricane, but definitely packing tropical storm winds and rain."

"And thunderstorms," added Meredith. "We'll see what we can find out before the storm hits, then get you over to B.J.'s house."

Bonnie Jean Waverly had been known as B.J. all her life, but while the name sounded colloquial enough, she and Malcolm Waverly had raised their girls with strong expectations. Julia and Wyatt both respected that. Cassie had fought the constraints of high expectations from the beginning. "Wyatt's coming without the family, so whatever we're discussing isn't kid-friendly. And now." She re-aimed her attention to the wall. "Let's see what we've got."

Meredith perched a hip on a stool and helped herself to a half sandwich. Carmen followed suit while Julia studied the timeline.

Meredith had taken pictures from the family photo albums Harlowe had given them. And when it came to the time in question, the four years of Lawrence's life, she'd left deliberate blanks.

Julia took out her phone and photographed the wall. "I want to be able to think about this tonight," she explained. "I do my best thinking late at night, when all is quiet. Carmen, have we found out any more on the nanny?"

"I did." Carmen set her sandwich down and picked up a couple of sheets of paper. "There's not a lot after she left her job with the Greens, but I did find that she moved north, married a Wisconsin farmer, and then nothing."

"Nothing?"

Carmen shook her head. "There are four children listed for the farmer, but their mother is listed as Gretchen, so where did Carolina go? Did she die in Wisconsin? I wasn't able to get county records, but I did contact a PI there to see if he could learn anything, because the snail mail process would have taken too long. He was reasonable about the cost," she added.

"That's a great idea." Meredith studied the timeline too. "Now if she happens to have left a diary of her actions...," she said with a dry note.

"Wouldn't that be convenient?" Carmen smiled. "Although unlikely."

"So where did they go on that vacation-turned-tragedy?" Meredith wondered out loud.

"No matter where they were, if there had been an accident, the press would have covered it." Julia said what all three were most likely thinking. "They would have been all over it if a rich Southerner's child met a tragic end on a northern vacation. So why wasn't it reported?"

"Because there was no accident," Meredith said. "Whatever happened to that precious little boy was a deliberate act, and it sickens me to think they got away with it. And that they lied to Harlowe and tried to skew his memories. His life. What kind of heartless people do that kind of thing?"

"Desperate ones," said Julia.

"But how do we prove it?" Carmen asked practically. "And if the goal is to protect Harlowe, aren't we verging on being just as guilty? As if this little boy doesn't deserve justice?"

"Justice is exactly what he'll get," said Julia firmly. "I know we want to protect Harlowe from what looks like a wretched truth, but we don't have that luxury."

"We don't," Meredith agreed. She breathed a sigh. "I've always believed that the truth will set us free, but I'm not so sure of it this time. I think the wrong people will suffer from this truth, and that's a crying shame, that two parents went to their graves getting off scot-free while their son has labored under this cloud all his life."

Carmen spoke up. "No one got off scot-free," she argued. "They didn't go to prison, but if you look into Patrice Green's eyes, you can see the sadness there. She suffered. But I'm amazed that they were able to pull this off with no one starting an investigation."

Julia exchanged looks with Meredith. "It wouldn't be the first time money talked," she said. "Maybe what happened to this boy got swept under the rug for the right price."

"Well, not to burst your bubbles, because you both seem set on this child being murdered, but death leaves bodies," Carmen noted in a somewhat cryptic voice. "And we don't have one. A body would make the news."

"Burial covers a lot of evidence," said Julia.

"So an accidental death and then the father runs to the hardware store and buys a shovel?" Carmen looked skeptical. "And even if the death wasn't accidental, did they have the presence of mind to take care of the body? And if this was Sully's love child, wouldn't he look more tragic in these later photos?" She pointed out the pictures from the mid 1920s. "And yet it's Patrice who seems to bear the weight of whatever happened. Or those later miscarriages, trying to have a boy. Trying to replace what she'd lost."

"Are we even the littlest bit further than we were when we started?" Meredith asked. "Because I'm still seeing circles. Not a path."

"We know where we need to fill in blanks." Julia pointed to the obvious gap in the photo timeline. "And we know that the photographer took the pictures, because we have one. But we also know that they were removed from Linkletter's collection, because they weren't there. So who did that? Sully? Patrice? Linkletter?"

"All three?" Carmen suggested.

"Let's take a drive and pose that very question to Martin," said Meredith. "Let's surprise him and ask him where the missing pictures are. He's a professional. He'll know those photo pages were adjusted. Let's see what he's got to say. And Carmen, do you mind double-checking county records for us? I want an extra pair of eyes on the standard things. Birth, death, anything to do with the Greens in that time frame. I know our first search came up blank, but let's cross-check with Netta Wilson. Even if that baby was born in a cottage, there should be some kind of record of his birth in that county. Netta could be listed as a Jane Doe or an assumed name. We can cross-reference. Then we can compare notes tomorrow."

"On it." Carmen rinsed the plates and put them in the dishwasher, then tucked the leftover sandwich in the fridge. "I'll keep you posted."

"And take my car." Julia tossed her the keys. "You can't drive forty minutes south with no AC in this heat. We'll call it the company car for the time being."

"I won't say no," Carmen declared with a nod to her phone. "Ninety-three degrees and climbing."

By the time Meredith and Julia got up to Charleston, the temperature was flirting with the upper nineties. "This puts glistening on a whole new level," Meredith grumbled as they slipped out of the car outside the younger Linkletter's home. They rang the bell. Knocked on the door. Then rang the bell again. "No one here?"

"But he's off for the summer," Meredith noted.

"Well, that doesn't mean he stays home the whole while," said Julia practically. "Let's check his wife's gallery."

"Good idea." They got back into the car, blasted the air-conditioning, and drove to the tucked-away gallery. When they walked through the front door, a very surprised Martin Linkletter stared at them. "You came back."

"We did, Mr. Linkletter, with just a few questions for you," Meredith stated in a firm voice. "Where are the missing pictures that were taken from the Greens' photo album? The ones having a certain little boy in them? In fact—" She whipped out the copied photo of Lawrence Green. "This little boy."

She'd told Julia to watch Linkletter's expression carefully, but careful consideration wasn't all that necessary when Martin Linkletter didn't just react.

He bolted out the back door, and by the time they got outside and crossed to Meredith's car, the photographer's great-grandson was racing away in a silver SUV.

Chapter Twenty

"WE NEED TO KNOW HOW Harlowe got hold of this picture, and we need to know it now," Julia declared as they headed back toward Savannah. She called Myla and explained that they needed to see the centenarian that day.

"He'll doze off right before dinner," Myla explained. "Then he'll be awake and take his walk around the square for forty minutes or so. Then he'll most likely turn on the old movie channel. His parents loved the movies and the theater," she explained. "He said it made them happy to see great productions on film and in town. They had a list of favorites, but the big musicals of the fifties and sixties topped the list. Harlowe loves them too. If you can get over here between the walk and the theatrical production, we should be good."

"We'll be there," Julia promised.

True to their word, Julia and Meredith walked down the street to Harlowe's house early that evening. They spotted him coming their way with his walker smacking the ground on every step.

"Ah, we caught you," Meredith exclaimed brightly. "My friend, we need to go inside and have a little conversation. It's an important one, and I don't want you to be overwhelmed, but we need to know a few things, and you're the only person alive who can help us. Shall we?" She motioned toward his house.

"This way," he told them then led the way to an inside elevator, just big enough for two. "I'll meet you upstairs," he told them, and when they went up the open stairway, they entered Harlowe's kitchen at the same time the elevator door slid open. Harlowe crossed the kitchen, then huffed when he settled onto one of the living room chairs facing the large-screen TV.

"I know walking is good for me, but walking mixed with heat and old age are not a good combination."

Myla brought him a tall glass filled with red liquid. She set it down right next to him and watched as he took a long, slow drink.

"Medicine?" Meredith whispered to her.

"Cheerwine," Myla replied. "We get cases of it from Kroger. It's Harlowe's version of a magic elixir."

"And a favorite of my husband's too," Julia told her.

Meredith smiled at Myla, then took the seat closest to Harlowe. Julia settled into a chair opposite him. Meredith slipped the copied photo from her bag. "Harlowe, there's something we absolutely need to know, and it could be crucial to solving this case. How did you get this picture, my friend?" She set the picture on his lap. "And how and why did you hide it for all these years?"

Harlowe traced the photo's outline with his old fingers. He raised his glass but then set it down without sipping. And then he sighed. "The book," he told them softly. "I took it out of his book."

"Whose book?" Julia asked.

"His, of course. We all had books," he added, but that only confused the issue further.

"Lawrence had a book?" Meredith pressed. She exchanged a look of question with Julia. "What kind of book?"

"One of them baby things. With all kinds of stuff in it. You know, with dates and pictures and locks of hair. Mama put them together. She'd paste this or that into it, and write things about us. Only, Lawrence's book was a mess. It used to be pretty, but when I saw it under Carolina's bed—"

"The nanny had the book?" Julia interrupted.

Harlowe gave a dark nod. "I dropped my sack of marbles, and I wasn't supposed to go into anyone's room, but one of my best aggies rolled into her room, so I crawled around on the floor, and when I pulled up the bottom of the bed covers, there was the aggie and Lawrence's book. It wasn't pretty like it used to be, though," he explained. "It made my hands dirty to handle it. That's why there's a mark on the picture I gave you, on the right-hand side. I smudged it. When I pulled out the book to see why it was dirty, that picture slipped out and I took it and hid it away. I don't know why, exactly, except that I missed my brother, and everybody was acting weird, and Mama was gone off to her room and no one saw her for a long while. Later I knew she'd have these spells and go off, hiding in her room, but I didn't know that back then. I just knew that she was gone, Lawrence was gone, and my daddy didn't laugh anymore. Then Bertha was born and that helped. She had a way with people from the get-go, if you get my drift. She was a bright light in a house full of darkness."

The poetry of the old man's words tugged at Julia, but she stayed on track. "But why would Carolina have that book stashed under her bed? And why was it dirty?"

"And why did she leave right then?" Meredith wondered aloud. "Harlowe, do you think Carolina had anything to do with Lawrence's disappearance?"

He shook his head firmly. "No, because she was here with Wilma. I think she was just as confused as I was," he told them. "She was the only one who didn't pretend he never existed, but then she was gone and the book was gone, and no one spoke of Lawrence again. Ever."

"I wonder if she took the book." Julia looked at Meredith.

Meredith raised both brows. "Did she run away and take the evidence with her?"

"And then disappeared up north," noted Julia.

"You found where she went?" Harlowe asked. "I never got even a hint of where she might have gone, and I don't know if she took the book or not. I just know she was gone, and it was gone, and I was the only one who remembered a funny and fearless little boy who used to climb trees and fences with me. I don't think I ever played that game again. It just wasn't the same without Lawrence. You know?"

Meredith's eyes looked moist as she covered his hand with hers. "I do know," she told him softly. "You've given us solid information, Harlowe, and we thank you. We'll get back to you as soon as—"

Julia's phone buzzed in her hand and she glanced down at the screen then up at Meredith. "Gotta go." She raised her phone and jumped out of her chair. "Someone broke into the office and went through the desks and the cabinets."

"But we're not even working there," said Meredith as she leaped out of her chair.

"I'm guessing they didn't know that, and somebody wants to make sure we don't figure this out," Julia replied. "I want to know who and why, because why would a hundred-year-old mystery worry anyone?"

This time Harlowe raised his gaze to hers. "Because the truth doesn't always set folks free, Judge. Sometimes it's the very thing that locks them up for a long, long time. A ruinous reputation isn't something one gets over quickly, and stains on a Southern family have a way of lasting."

Stains on a Southern family.

The Linkletters' multigenerational tribute.

Martin's desire to have his exhibit turned into a documentary.

She took Meredith's hand and hurried her toward the door. "I know what's going on." She whispered the words so Harlowe wouldn't overhear. No sense getting the old fellow's hopes up. "I don't know the stakes, but I'm pretty sure I know why someone's getting in our way, and it all comes down to a certain photographer's reputation. I'm pretty sure Martin's great-grandpa was involved, or at least knowledgeable, and if Martin loses this documentary deal, that's a whole lot of cash that disappears in one moment of truth. And people who are low on cash are willing to do desperate things."

"And his wife said it was hard to find customers in the summer." Meredith scrunched up her face as they tried to hurry to the car, but the increasing wind fought them every step of the way. "I thought it was just casual conversation, but you're right. If we turn up with Martin Linkletter's great-grandfather being involved in a crime, no one's going to pay big bucks for that legacy of the South. And speaking of Martin," she breathed as shadows deepened around them. "There he is! And he's aiming for us!"

Sure enough, behind the wheel of a silver SUV was Martin Linkletter, and he was steering that SUV right at them!

Chapter Twenty-One

THERE WAS NO TIME TO reach Meredith's car and get in. "Sidewalk," said Julia, and she darted down the narrow path separating the elaborate rowhouses.

"And police," Meredith breathed as she pulled her phone out of her pocket.

Julia heard Meredith give a grunt of frustration. "My phone's dead!" she exclaimed. She didn't sound all that out of breath, so maybe that step-counting nonsense wasn't all that bad an idea, Julia decided. She whipped out her own phone and dialed 911.

"Please send someone to Troup Square—East Charlton Street— there's a guy chasing us in an SUV." Julia got her message across to the dispatcher, then hit Carmen's speed dial. When Carmen answered, she yelled, "We're running down East Charlton—Linkletter is chasing us in his SUV—I've called 911!" She didn't wait for Carmen to answer; she knew the dispatcher expected her to stay on the line. She switched back to that call. She was out of breath and could barely pant out which house they were now in front of. Tomorrow she would definitely start counting steps.

She looked up. Massive clouds darkened the area. The intensity increased as the tropical storm winds wreaked havoc with the trees, the bushes, and the women's hair.

The thickly shaded streets deepened the growing darkness, and as thunder rumbled loudly to their south, fresh lightning crackled to their right. "This is going to be a humdinger," Meredith hollered.

She was right, and they didn't dare lead Martin Linkletter into an innocent person's house for shelter. How long would it take the police to get there? Five minutes? Ten? A half hour, with the storm and growing road debris?

"We've got to get to the car and lead him away from here," Julia told Meredith.

"We'll never make it in time, here he comes!" Meredith shrieked as Martin's car took the far corner in true racing form. "Back around the houses," she yelled as she sprinted ahead.

They would never be able to keep ahead of this man on foot, they couldn't seek shelter at anyone's home, and no way was Julia going to head away from civilization—

They darted left. "This way!" Meredith pushed to the front and Julia let her take lead. This was her turf. Her neighborhood. If there was a place to hide, she'd know it.

The rain began.

Not a gentle summer rain, pattering through the trees, but an all-out onslaught, sheeting the streets and the lovely intricate homes forming the square. Young trees bent under the storm's fury. Old trees spewed cracking limbs, and Julia shrieked in surprise when one landed so close to her that the thin upper branches scraped her face and her left arm.

Her heart hammered.

Her breath caught.

Never in her life had she ever had to truly fear for her life. Today—right now—she did.

She was almost out of breath when Meredith grabbed her hand and spun her into a space behind a big heavy door.

The smell of gasoline and motor oil hit Julia. Darkness surrounded them, and when Meredith directed Julia's hand to the thick-handled door in front of them, Julia got her drift despite the lack of light. She braced her feet and clung tight to the door, holding it shut.

Would Linkletter think it was locked?

She hoped so. She hoped he'd try it, realize it wasn't budging, then move on, searching for them in the storm's wrath.

The pressure came right then. The pressure of someone trying to pull open the heavy wooden door between them. Julia felt it through her hands, and the door budged slightly.

Was it enough to clue him into their hiding spot?

She hoped not. Prayed not. But she kept her prayers silent petitions, hoping Martin Linkletter's quest would take him away from the door. Away from them.

The pressure on the door lightened. She breathed a sigh of relief and loosened her grip.

The moment she did, the door wrenched open and there he was, soaked to the skin, looking deranged and shrieking, "You've ruined it. Everything! You foolish old women, you've absolutely, positively ruined everything!"

Old?

Foolish?

Nobody got to call Julia old and foolish. Ever. She faced him down, knowing she could protect herself and Meredith if need be.

He looked desperate. And kind of sad too.

But mostly desperate and dangerous, and Julia was just about to withdraw the small firearm she'd never pulled before, when lights and sirens came screeching their way. The quick-moving police force saved her the trouble as they swarmed in and took Martin Linkletter into custody.

But the last thing Julia saw was the expression of utter sadness the man aimed their way.

Not anger.

Utter dejection. And that look made her question what they'd done, and maybe, what they were about to do. Maybe—just maybe, she thought—they shouldn't reopen this investigations business, because Julia wasn't sure her tightly strung emotions could stand it.

And then Chase Bellefontaine appeared.

He reached out an arm to his mother, and one to Julia, and tugged them both into his embrace. And when he released them, with rain pelting his back and the cavernous vault for lawn equipment gaping behind them, he said, "I'm impressed, ladies. And wet. And I took a blow to the head when I got to the house, Mom, and let me just say, that new housekeeper packs a wallop."

"Carmen?" Julia stared at him.

"She hit you?" Meredith's eyes popped wide.

"She's not a housekeeper," Julia told him. "She's our Gal Friday. Our office manager. Our go-to person for just about everything."

"Well, your Gal Friday had just pulled peach upside-down cake out of the oven when she brandished a rolling pin to protect herself and all your worldly goods," said Chase. "Lucky for me it was a glancing blow."

"Oh, darling." Meredith pulled him into a hug. "Are you all right? Really?"

"Fine, just bumped and bruised. And don't go firing her over this, either. She was just doing her job."

"Fire her?" Meredith lifted her brows again as the police chief motioned her over. "We'll give her a raise. How many employees would go to such lengths to protect us? And our stuff? And you didn't say you were coming," she reminded him. "Otherwise I would have warned her."

"I'll make sure I call her the next time," he promised, and the amused glimmer in his eye said he wasn't nearly as upset about the whole thing as Julia would be if she'd been the object of a rolling pin attack.

Julia's phone chimed in a text and a voice mail right then.

One from her mother, wondering what caused her delay—

And one from Carmen, and when she heard the note of excitement in Carmen's voice, Julia realized that Wyatt and her mother were going to have to solve the current Cassie-dilemma alone. Because Carmen had stumbled onto amazingly big news.

News that changed everything.

Vermont
Spring 1937

"You do know about making cheese." Willis came into the lean-to at the near side of the barn and whistled softly when he spotted the cheese pans lining the shelf. The spring influx of milk brought Caroline an abundance of cheese-making opportunities. "You said you'd watched kids, but you must have grown up on a dairy farm to be this good at setting curd."

"It's a learned skill, for sure." She hedged the truth like she'd been doing for the past eight months. "Hannah has no thought for it, but Clara delves in repeatedly, wanting to know more. She's got a keen interest, that one."

"While my Hannah dreams of this and that and the other thing. Jane told me she'd need a good marriage or a better education, and I expect she's right, although with Hannah's good grades, she could teach school when she graduates. Maybe that would give her a solid footing and room for stories. Jane was of a mind that stories were important. Said they eased the mundane, and I suppose an old farm is the definition of mundane." His smile said he wasn't offended by his late wife's beliefs.

"Hannah's got a good head on her shoulders and a ripe imagination to go alongside. She'll be fine. And she turns more than one young man's head at Sunday gatherings."

"I noticed the same thing," he admitted. "But I'm not in a hurry to have her gone. She's young in some ways, yet, and marriage isn't an easy road."

His words piqued her as she repeatedly rinsed and drained a new batch of curd. "But you and your wife did well, didn't you?"

"We got on well after a fashion," he told her frankly. "We had eyes for each other when we were young, but her father made us wait until Jane was nineteen, and it seemed like so long. And I wasn't all that smart about women back then, so it took a while for things to iron out. I expect that's normal, but it ain't something we men sit around and jaw about. Unlike you women."

His tone inspired her smile. "We are more talkative."

"I figured it was necessary when you've got so much to do, so many jobs, so many children, and all their fussing about this and that. I'd be set to lose my patience, and Jane would make things right in a quiet voice that rang out like a peal of thunder for all its soft tone. She'd speak firmly, and those kids would hop to. She said yes when she meant yes and no when she didn't, and they figured out she meant it. That wasn't me doing that. It was all Jane."

"You loved her."

His expression stilled. Then he nodded. "We had it good. Went both ways. And she wasn't afraid to scold me that if anything ever happened to her, I was to go on living. Find someone else. Give these children a mother."

What kind of woman did that kind of thing? A strong one, she realized. "I think all things happen in God's time, Will. It's we who get impatient, pushing it."

"And you, Caroline?"

When had he moved closer? Close enough that his scent wrapped around her, a bit of hay and stable and rugged soap.

"Do you get impatient?"

She met his gaze and read his look, and her heart began beating harder. Stronger. She did get impatient, and she did dream sometimes, and lately those dreams had been about him. About them. But they were dreams with no future, because she knew what he didn't, that she had a husband and child half-a-country away. "I don't dare," she whispered in return, but when he laid his big hand on her cheek, she longed to turn into it. Turn into him. And yet the contemplation of sin drew her back. "There's much you don't know about me, Will."

"Ready to listen." He slipped his hand along her cheek once more, and the feel of it seemed right. So right. But she alone knew it was wrong. "Tell me about you, Caroline. I want to hear all the stories."

Impossible.

Was it? Was it impossible to tell a good man, a man she'd learned to trust, the truth and let him be the judge?

Fear took hold. A raw fear, thinking of how he might react to her words. A child, lost in suspicious circumstances, and her a party to it. A marriage and child she'd walked away from, leaving no trace. That right there would put a pause on his pursuit, for a man who'd loved well would not want to risk a woman who runs away. She stepped back. "If told, you would have a different opinion of me, Will, and I can't abide that, so I'll keep my silence and be your friend.

And a true friend accepts the quiet as part of the friendship."

"And a man who sees sorrow in his beloved is willing to take the time to unlock that sorrow. Day by day. Season by season. There's no hurry, Caroline."

Her heart stuttered.

She should leave his employ before this went further. She knew that the look she read in his eye was reflected in her own longing, and yet it could come to nothing.

Still she stayed, tempting fate, because if only for a short while, the thought of the true love of a man like Willis Blodgett was too great a temptation to shrug off. And truth to tell, she didn't want to shrug him off. Not in the least.

Chapter Twenty-Two

THEY HURRIED OVER TO MEREDITH's house once the police got the gist of Linkletter's offenses. Julia and Meredith rushed through the back door. Chase followed at a more leisurely pace then pretended to scout the area before stepping inside.

Carmen spotted him and froze. "I am so sorry," she began as Chase made it a point to come through the door carefully, as if avoiding a confrontation. "I can't believe I hit you, Mr. Bellefontaine. Please forgive me for doing such a thing." Carmen was rarely humble and contrite, but tonight she was both of those things. Julia was about to reassure her when Chase paused. Folded his arms. Pretended to think the situation over.

Carmen's expression changed.

She'd been humble.

Now, watching Meredith's son weigh his response, Carmen lowered her brows. Her eyes flashed. And she squared her shoulders and met his gaze. "Of course when one arrives anywhere unexpectedly, one should expect the unexpected," she declared.

"The fact that I have a key should make a difference, I would think," he countered.

"A key that I was not made aware of until after I defended myself," she shot back.

"Fortunately, your aim was off."

Surprise widened Carmen's big brown eyes. "On the contrary, my aim was perfect. You blocked the attempt successfully," she replied.

"Defensive tackle for four very busy years. Go Dawgs," he explained. His voice was almost nonchalant, and while Julia was soaked to the skin, she wasn't blind. There was a sparkle in Chase's eyes as he faced off with Carmen, and it wasn't anything she'd ever seen before.

"Then I'm fortunate you didn't use any foolish football holds on me, I suppose, as I struggled to protect myself and my employer from a break-in."

He stared at her.

She stared back.

And then she swallowed. Hard. As if—

A smile eased over Chase's face. As his look softened, he extended a hand. "Let's start again, shall we?"

Carmen looked at him, then the hand, then him again.

"I'm Chase Bellefontaine. My mom lives here. And thank you for taking such good care of her."

For a few short seconds Carmen stayed silent. Then she reached out. Took his hand. And for a brief moment, neither one said a word. Not one blessed word.

Then Carmen lowered her chin slightly. "It is a pleasure to meet you, Mr. Bellefontaine."

"Chase," he corrected instantly. "Just Chase."

"And I am Carmen Lopez," she replied. And still, for about four more seconds, their hands connected.

Meredith had gone through to the nearby bath for towels. She flipped one to Chase and one to Julia, oblivious to what had just played out in her kitchen.

"I am unaccustomed to running for my life in sandals," Meredith lamented as they all began to towel off.

The doorbell rang.

Carmen hurried that way, then came back a moment later with a big pan of food—

And Julia's mother, B.J.

"Mom." Julia jumped up. Her mother was eighty-four years old but had the constitution and drive of someone twenty years younger. "I'm sorry I had to miss dinner."

"Wyatt and I got it all worked out, so no concern needed, and I knew," exclaimed B.J., "that you wouldn't have missed anything concerning Wyatt and me if it wasn't absolutely necessary. I brought lasagna and garlic bread, and if you gals have stuff to talk about, I'll go ahead and heat things up. Hello, Chase, so good to see you!" She beamed when she saw Meredith's younger son off to the left. "And don't you look absolutely wonderful?"

Chase was wet from top to bottom. He laughed, slung the towel around his shoulders, and motioned upstairs. "Good to see you too, Mrs. Waverly. I'm going to head up and get changed."

"Me too," said Meredith. "Julia, come on, I know my stuff will be a little big on you, but it'll be dry and comfortable. Let's get changed while B.J. warms things up, and then"—she aimed a look at Carmen—"I want to listen to everything you've got to say, dear girl. And if there's a hot meal at the same time?" she continued. "All the better."

Reverend Bowman was a godly man. He oversaw the small church in the quaint village, and he had an understanding heart. Perhaps if she went to him for advice, he could help her see her path more clearly. Would he stay silent on the matter? Keep her confidence?

She didn't know, and when his wife came by to learn cheese-making skills the following week, Caroline posed the question to her. "Anne, I'm in need of counsel."

"Oh, dearie, aren't we all?" Anne Bowman smiled at her over her rimless glasses. "How can I help?"

Such kind words, with no expectation attached. "I need advice, and I thought your Thomas might be a good source. It is a delicate matter that needs to be kept private."

Anne knit her brow. "Some delicate matters can be fixed with a ceremony and a ring, child. It can be that easy."

"Oh, Anne." Heat flamed her cheeks instantly. "It's not that. Well, it is, but not as you think, and I don't want to trouble the reverend if it will forever change his opinion of me. Does that make sense?"

"Being well regarded is a fine thing, but it's more import-ant that God hold us in high regard, Caroline. People are quick to judge these days. I expect it's always been that way and ever shall be," she continued, "but it's the Lord's opinion we hold dear. Not that of mankind. And yet here, on earth, that can be the most vexing."

"Exactly. And it's not that I'm proud of what I've done, but I can't move forward with this weight on my soul, and I don't know how to shift it properly."

Anne was rinsing curd. She paused and peered at Caroline again. "If I am privy to your concerns, there shall be no sharing and no malice, for it should always be that way among women of faith. I will tell you honestly that my husband is bound by church laws. There are times he should have stepped around them and never has, for fear of those above him. I think you need to know that before you approach him."

"I see." Caroline wrapped cheesecloth around a firm circle of Vermont cheddar. "That is quite important to know, isn't it?"

"Yes, child." Anne frowned in sympathy. "But I am under no such binding, Caroline. I can hear people's words and kindly keep them to myself. Give advice or take it, and I am not required to act on it. The glory of being a pastor's wife and not the pastor himself."

"But don't you share everything with him?" Caroline asked, and she was relieved when the older woman shook her head.

"I share as needed, and I'm quite capable of keeping my own counsel as a woman, a friend, and a wife and mother. Few men comprehend the intricacies of womanhood and motherhood. If you want to share with me, it will go no further. But I would never coerce you."

Caroline pulled the cloth tight.

Her hands shook, but the cloth's pressure disguised that. Did she need to tell both stories?

No. The first had no bearing on anything now, did it? And the book was safely tucked beneath clothing on a strong wooden shelf. But the second chapter— "I was married once."

Anne said nothing, but her eyebrows shifted up.

"It could have been a beautiful marriage, but he was more in love with the land than with his wife."

"A farmer, then?"

Caroline nodded then realized she needed to tell both stories. And when it came to naming their son, Anne shook her head firmly. "To take the right of naming away from the mother is a grievous thing. And of course had you told him about the lost child..."

"He would have insisted I go to the police and lodge a complaint, and I couldn't do that. I can't imagine either parent hurting a child, and they were suffering enough."

"So you were willing to protect them even though they sacked you."

"It makes no sense, I know."

"On the contrary, it makes perfect sense." Anne had set her curd aside. Now she reached out a hand to Caroline. "You loved them. The parents. The children."

"I did, and I felt so sorry for Patrice, the sadness weighed her so. But then I worried that my love might be blocking me from the truth, that maybe someone did hurt Lawrence and I should have spoken up."

"Do you truly think they did?"

She shook her head swiftly. "I do not. But not knowing leads me to conjecture, and my mind spins in so many directions. But to bring more grief to an already grieving family seemed wrong."

"You have a good heart, child. A very good heart, and while I can't speak to the situation in Savannah other than offer my deepest condolence for such a thing to come to pass, I can find answers in Wisconsin. If he has followed through with divorce, it will be public record and that can be discovered. I will not use your name and can have the inquiry come from my sister in Pennsylvania. In that way, no one will find you here, if that is your wish. But are you sure that is your desire? There is no lost feeling for your husband?"

"There used to be. For the way he was before he listened to his mother's words. He cared for me then. Perhaps he has found a stronger wife. A better mother for Lawson. And maybe one strong enough to stand up to his mother, for that was something I could not do."

"I shall send an inquiry quickly, but these things take time. And in the meantime I will pray that God comforts your soul. That He offers the peace of His kingdom for your well-being."

"I will take your help and your prayers with a grateful heart." Caroline whispered the words. "And Anne?"

The older woman met her gaze.

"Thank you."

Compassion warmed the older woman's face. "You are most welcome."

Chapter Twenty-Three

"IT'S ALL RIGHT HERE IN black and white," Carmen explained while B.J. heated the food a few minutes later. She handed Julia and Meredith each a printed sheet from one of the ancestry sites. Chase came up behind Julia and read over her shoulder as Carmen took a seat across from them.

Meredith shrieked first.

She stared at the notation, then Carmen, then the notation again. "I don't believe this."

Julia came to the same point at that moment. "This is impossible."

"Except it's not," Carmen said softly. "In fact, if you go back a generation, things become remarkably clear. It's just that no one in the local family has gone into this history, a history that means nothing now but would have had catastrophic results back then."

"I'm gobsmacked," Julia whispered.

"Me too." Meredith studied the test results and swallowed hard. "All these years of worry. And loss."

"For nothing." Julia couldn't take her eyes off the paper.

"Not for nothing," Meredith corrected her gently. "Back then it would have been very different. It would have never been the same for any of them."

Julia rubbed her hands together. "I can't wait until we go see Harlowe and explain things to him. He is not going to believe this."

"But what about this guy trying to kill you both?" Carmen demanded. "Why was he doing that?"

Meredith shook her head. "I have no idea, but tomorrow we're going to find out. We'll see Harlowe, and we'll confront Martin Linkletter at the jail and see what's going on, because there are still things we don't know."

"And we can stop worrying that Jem Baldwin is going to blow the family out of the water with his book, because we're about to hand him his newest best seller," said Julia. "And I can't say I'm sorry about that. He turned out to be one of the good guys after all."

"And you guys only had to hide away from a crazed person once with this investigation, so that's good." Chase deadpanned the statement, then reached out and bumped knuckles with Meredith, then Julia. "Well done."

He grinned at Julia, and the concern that had risen to choke her a short time ago faded.

"Food first," B.J. said as she crossed to the table with loaded plates. "When I heard that you two were in hot water, I decided that I have one daughter who is always begging my help and another one who never asks for anything. While the squeaky wheel gets the grease, the hardworking daughter gets dinner."

"Delivered by the most wonderful mother in the world," Julia said. She sighed as she took a deep breath of the scent of cheesy pasta. "This smells absolutely perfect and gives us time to figure out the hows and the whys, now that we have the what."

"That's what mothers are for, darling."

Anne crossed the barn on quiet feet. She slipped a folded sheet of paper from her sleeve and quietly handed it to Caroline.

A decree of divorce was granted to Hans Martin Engstrom in Green County, Wisconsin, on charge of abandonment by his wife and mother of their child, Lawson Engstrom, September of 1936. No trace of mother had been found despite diligent efforts on the part of husband.

The paper was signed and dated several months before.

He had divorced her.

Caroline didn't expect to feel pain. She was the one who walked away, after all, but seeing the words in print hit her hard.

"I'm sorry, dear." Anne settled an arm around Caroline's shoulders. They'd met in the cheese-making lean-to again, as privacy was unheard of in the busy, child-filled farmhouse. "I can see this comes as a shock."

Tears stung Caroline's eyes.

She brushed them back and shook her head. "Not so much a shock as a disappointment. That's foolish, isn't it?" She dashed another round of tears from her cheeks and faced Anne.

"Why would your disappointment be foolish? A marriage is a precious thing to lose and should be grieved as much as a loss of life. Here, now." She handed Caroline a soft, clean

towel. "I have no hanky present and should have thought to bring one, but this will suffice."

Caroline pressed the cool cotton to her face and sat straighter. "He didn't come for me."

Anne nodded, understanding.

"Even though I supposed he never would, that he'd realize I wasn't the wife he needed or wanted, part of me hoped that something in him would send him looking for me. That he might show up one day and pledge his love for me again."

"And that didn't happen." Anne didn't speak to the obvious, that Caroline had hidden herself well, since they both understood that a man who truly loved his wife wouldn't have taken his mother's side in everything, and honestly, would have come looking. "But this gives you freedom to make choices you couldn't make before. After you tell Willis, of course."

Tell Willis. It had been hard enough to reveal the truth to Anne, a gentle and kind friend, but just a friend. Did she dare risk sullying Willis's good opinion of her? He was a good man, but a godly one too. Would he understand the tangles of her heart? "I could keep my silence. Not rock the boat."

Anne cringed. "Can a strong marriage begin on the seeds of deceit? I think not."

"Leaving out a piece of truth isn't the same as lying."

"A sin of omission is still a sin, dear girl." Anne drew a deep breath. "But I pledged my silence and it is, of course, up to you. But a former marriage and a child aren't the kind of secrets a good woman keeps, Caroline."

She knew that. She knew that before the words came out of Anne's mouth, but that didn't make her task easier.

When the children went off to school a few weeks later, she prayed her hardest and summoned what little courage she had. And then she headed out to find Willis in the big barn.

Oh that smile, the moment he saw her. With a craggy face and deep-set eyes, he wasn't what some would term an overly handsome man, but the kindness he exuded made him quite good-looking in her eyes. "Did you need help with something, Caroline?"

She shook her head and moved toward him, trying to calm the nervous flutters within. "You asked about my story."

"I did." He set down the tool he'd been using on the old horse-drawn plow. His face searched hers, and he seemed to realize she needed to go slowly, and that deepened her affection for him, but he hadn't heard her words yet, and that patience could fly right out the barn window in a few moments.

"I was married once."

He stood still. Perfectly still. "As was I."

"But you lost your beloved wife unexpectedly. It wasn't that way with me, Willis." She pulled in a breath and folded her hands to quiet their shaking. It didn't work. "I left my husband and son. He then divorced me. I abandoned them *and walked away and didn't tell them where I was going. I just—left."*

His eyes searched her face for answers. "He hurt you."

"No."

"He scorned you?"

Not overtly. She shook her head.

"You left a child behind?" She felt the pain in his words. She knew how it sounded. It sounded horrid because it was horrid, and yet despite her misgivings, Anne was right. The story needed to be told.

And then his next question set the stage she'd feared all along, because Willis, with all his kind ways, didn't ask why she left…

He asked how she could have done such a thing, and in that moment she knew what was about to happen and that she had no choice but to travel the new path she'd just chosen. "His mother was more my child's mother than I was. And the decisions made for the farm or our time or our lives didn't include me. It got so nothing included me, and I had to leave."

Confusion pushed his compassion aside. "You didn't talk to him, Caroline? Explain yourself and your feelings? Take charge of your child the way a mother would do? The way you do here with Hannah, Clara, Charles, and Lia?"

"It was not allowed." She breathed out softly. "It would never be allowed, Willis."

"I see." He brought his hand to his chin and stroked the short whiskers there, but she knew he didn't see, that it

sounded thin in the telling. Why did something that loomed so harsh in the moment seem pathetic in explanation?

"I needed to tell you. To be honest with you."

His eyebrows shot up. "After all this time."

She wanted to argue that. To explain that she was entitled to her privacy, like anyone, but she didn't. Once again she stayed quiet. She stared at him.

He stared back.

And when she turned to go back to the house to work, his voice made her pause. "Caroline."

She turned, not daring to hope, but longing to hope. "Yes?"

"You will need to leave, of course."

Leave? She took a step back. "Haven't I done a fine job here?"

"Yes. We both know that, but I cannot have a divorced woman caring for my children. What kind of example would that be? What kind of lesson does that teach?"

Her heart sank. She'd weighed the likelihood that his feelings would be shelved after learning the truth, but to lose the job she loved? A job she was good at? This seemed grossly unfair. "They have no need to know."

"But I know." He stood firm and still, as if the wrongs she'd committed were unforgivable. "And how can I present you to my children as a woman of faith when you've broken sacred vows? And then deceived us about them?"

This time she folded her arms and stood her ground. "I have deceived no one, and you know it, Willis Blodgett.

I came here for work. Nothing more. My personal life was none of your business. You made it your business by flirting with me."

His mouth dropped open, then he shut it, as if he knew it was true.

"You were kind and compassionate and spoke of longing and futures. What you meant was as long as it was on your terms and your standards. How grossly unfair of you." She moved back and refused to cry. That could be done later. Much later. "Have you no secrets, Willis? No youthful offenses?" A slight wince said she'd guessed correctly. "I hope for your sake that God is more forgiving of you than you are of others. I will pack my things and be gone shortly."

She wheeled around, her long skirt slashing the hay mound to her left. Hay dust filled the air, and that's what she would remember as she headed for the door she'd left ajar. Willis, standing there, his hands stuffed in his pockets, watching her through a thin veil of sun-soaked bits of hay.

Chapter Twenty-Four

"JAIL FIRST," MEREDITH SAID THE next morning.

"Before we see Harlowe?" Julia didn't try to hide her surprise. "Don't we owe it to him to reassure him first thing?"

Meredith agreed but added a caveat. "Yes, but he's at the foot doctor this morning and won't be back until nearly eleven. Let's use this block of time to see what's going on with Martin Linkletter. If they'll let us talk to him."

They did, and when Julia and Meredith were ushered into a small, colorless room, the history teacher faced them head-on. "I'm sorry." He looked at Meredith, then Julia, then Meredith again. "I don't know what got into me. It wasn't just the lure of the money from the production company. We're not rich by any means, and the money would be a big help with my kids' college loans. It was the thought of finally seeing my great-grandfather's legacy achieve the acclaim it's deserved, with that one foolish exception on his part. And why he would be part of some kind of cover-up, I don't know, but I couldn't believe he ever did anyone harm. Not a man who risked his good name by making sure the harshness of the times was recorded for posterity. In a quiet way, of course."

"Because if he'd been bolder, his business would have been targeted," Meredith suggested.

Martin nodded. "He was a historian first and a photographer second. He's got some hidden shots that he gleaned over the years. Amazing shots. But now it will all be tainted because he hid evidence for Sully Green. One mistake, that long ago, and it all comes crashing down."

He looked bereft.

Meredith and Julia exchanged looks. "What if it didn't come crashing down?"

He knit his brow.

"What if instead of being a conspirator to a crime, your great-grandfather was really saving multiple people from a life of scorn and shunning?"

The W between his eyes knit deeper. "I don't understand. I know what happened back then, at least my great-grandfather's part in it. He told my grandpa, and my grandpa shared it with me, how he took out photos of a little boy and gave them to his father. And it wasn't just the ones that were in the family pages," he confessed. "Granddad said there were several others that were more general, and he gave them all back to wipe the slate clean."

"A clean slate isn't always a bad thing," Julia noted. "A lot of folks like to start over with a clean slate, don't they?"

"They do." He drew a deep breath, then sighed. "When the public television network came to me about making a documentary of the old South, featuring Great-Granddad's work, I knew it was a good thing. He knew the people and captured them on film. It wasn't just photography. It was art. But then all of a sudden that Baldwin guy was talking on cable about research for his next book, and how Savannah's secrets and the Green family were all going to be major components, and all I could see was this documentary falling apart, and all because my great-grandfather helped cover up a dreadful accident. An accident that maybe wasn't so accidental, after all."

"Exactly what we thought," Julia explained to him. "But we were wrong, and so are you. Mr. Linkletter, we can't get you out of trouble completely. You grossly overreacted."

Meredith perked up as if suddenly realizing a truth. "You stole Baldwin's laptop."

He nodded. "I didn't do anything to it, I just needed to slow him down."

"You tried to scare us off by having someone pay a homeless man to plant a picture of Lawrence with a threatening note written on it."

"But I didn't really threaten anything," he said.

"And it did buy an elderly man a lot of good meals," Meredith conceded.

"So that ended up all right," Julia agreed. "Although you did trash our offices."

He shook his head vehemently. "I looked at files but found nothing, and believe me, your offices were a mess before I slipped in the side door with a deliveryman. I don't know how anyone can work like that," he added. "How do you two find stuff?"

Julia wasn't about to give him an explanation he didn't deserve. She stared right at him and leaned forward. "Were you really going to run us down with your car?"

He shook his head. "Of course not. I'm not a monster. But I wanted to stop you. And talk to you. I saw you in the art gallery, and

I panicked. It was stupid. I thought if I could just talk to you—I'm sorry," he added softly. "I wanted to protect Great-Granddad's legacy and my own reputation as a historian and teacher. And now I've gone off the deep end and messed it all up."

Julia wasn't sure he had, but this wasn't her jurisdiction so she stayed quiet about that while she addressed the other issue—Martin's family history. "We want you to know that your great-grandfather did nothing wrong, Martin. There was no crime. The documentary should move forward. So should Jem Baldwin's book. They both have an amazing story to tell. A story we need to share with Harlowe Green." She stood and signaled the guard. He moved forward and motioned for Martin to stand.

He did.

"We'll talk again, but I want you to know that I forgive you," Meredith told him, and the transformation on his face was a revelation to Julia. "I'm glad no one was hurt, and I'll be praying for you. You're a good man, Martin. I've known that from the beginning."

They got outside, and Julia paused Meredith with a hand to her arm. Their eyes met. "You absolved him."

"Well, not the criminal intent. That's up to the law," Meredith explained. And then she gave Julia a gentle smile. "But he got my personal absolution, and sometimes that's enough to keep someone's head above water in hard times. Just knowing someone isn't holding a grudge can be absolutely freeing, can't it?"

Julia thought of her long-held angst over her scatterbrained sister. "I expect it can."

Meredith tapped her watch. "Harlowe gets home in an hour. Let's see if Maggie Lu is available for a quick chat, then we'll go see

Harlowe. She said something the other day that didn't hit me then, but makes a great deal of sense now."

"'It's there, in that sweet child's face,'" whispered Julia. "She looked at Lawrence and she knew, didn't she?"

"When you spend your life seeing patterns come and go, it probably comes to you more quickly," Meredith answered. They texted Maggie Lu.

She was home and told them to come right over.

They climbed into Meredith's SUV and drove to Maggie Lu's little bungalow on Le Grand. They were able to park just up the road and walk back.

Maggie Lu welcomed them at the door. "Justine dropped off lemon cookies yesterday, so I have a plate of them waiting." She showed the ladies into a clean and well-appointed kitchen. "Granny Luv always said that a few good rooms are as good as a palace, and she was right about that. Now, what is it you lovely ladies need?"

"Your wisdom," said Meredith. She slipped Lawrence's picture out of the pocket of her bag. "You saw this picture and said it's there, right there, in his face. What did you mean?"

Maggie Lu wasted no time. "This child is beautiful, the best of two worlds," she told them gently. "But my guess is that those two worlds would not have been understanding or forgiving a hundred years ago. And while I wouldn't have looked at her mama and seen the same thing, this little one's features are not unfamiliar to people of color."

"Would people then have known? Like you did?"

She shook her head. "I don't expect so, especially since the Green family has dark Irish on their side, and it's probably the combination that highlights this child's African heritage. The right mix of science and fate. But what happened to him?" she asked softly. "Please don't tell me that evil befell this beautiful child."

"Not the kind of evil we can punish, unfortunately," Meredith told her. "Patrice must have feared that people would figure things out. They took him north and gave him away, rather than let people speculate about Patrice's family."

"Would they have?" asked Julia. "I guess that's what I need to know to come to peace with all of this. Would people have looked at this child and known he was part black?" She sighed. "Or did a fragile mother panic?"

"Well, there's truth in both of those statements, and times being what they were, who was going to take a chance?" Maggie Lu asked them directly. "It wasn't as if folks would just shrug their shoulders and say 'Oh, all right, Mr. Sullivan Green went and married himself a black woman.'" She faced both women frankly. "You know the figures, how a drop of black blood made you black and blocked you from all opportunity that white folks enjoyed."

"But what brought this to a head?" Meredith asked. The moment she said it, Julia saw the truth in the timing.

"Her mother's death," she whispered. "Either her mother told her on her deathbed, or Patrice discovered the truth as she was caring for her."

"Birthing and dying are a time for confession and absolution," Maggie Lu said softly. "They loosen a tongue, that's for certain."

"Maggie Lu, thank you." Meredith stood up and hugged Maggie Lu, then Julia followed suit. "Your insight is such a huge help to us. I studied that picture ten ways to Sunday and didn't see the obvious until it was pointed out to me, but life has given you a whole other perspective and it's a blessing to us. Both of us," she added with a nod in Julia's direction. "We have to go see Harlowe and explain things. We'll see you soon."

"Lord willing, and I'll look forward to it," Maggie Lu answered.

The women crossed the porch, went down the steps and the walk, and approached the car quietly. But when they got to the vehicle, Meredith checked an incoming text and sent Julia a satisfied smile. "Let's get right over there. I can't wait to show him this whole thing. And he says he wants Jem there too, and Jem just texted that he's on his way."

In an odd, roundabout way it seemed right to have him in on the conversation.

Chapter Twenty-Five

AT 11:05 MYLA THOMAS USHERED Julia and Meredith into the front room of Harlowe's home. A few minutes later, Jem Baldwin joined them. He had a black leather satchel in one hand. He came into the room, and Julia was hard-pressed to describe the look on his face. Part resignation, part expectation, but there was an undefinable sadness too. An emotion she'd seen hinted before.

Meredith took a seat at Harlowe's right, and Julia sat in a comfortable chair nearby. Jem chose a seat on Harlowe's left, opposite Julia. He set the bag down, folded his hands, and waited.

"Thank you for coming over." Harlowe faced the writer directly, and for an aged man, he showed great strength. "I wanted you to be here to hear whatever the women have to say. I know that the way things are today, secrets come out. Things don't stay hidden the way they used to, and maybe that's a God-thing. It might be good that the time for secrets is over, but I didn't want a stranger to find this out."

Jem raised his hands, appearing confused. "I don't understand."

Meredith held up the picture of Lawrence.

Jem stared at it. Then swept them each a glance. Then he swallowed hard. "Lawrence."

Shock darkened Harlowe's face. "You know about him."

"I know of him," the author confessed. "But nothing really about him. I'd love to hear you tell the story."

Harlowe's hands were shaking. He reached for his ever-present glass. Meredith helped him steady it while he took a long sip, then she set the glass back down for him.

He cleared his throat, then started talking. "He disappeared when I was small, and I asked Meredith and Judge Foley to find out what happened to him. That was their commission, and they're here to tell us what they've found. After ninety-nine years, I will finally know where my brother went, what happened to him. And why I was never allowed to mention his name again."

Jem's expression of empathy seemed to understand more than Julia would have thought possible, and she watched both men as Meredith began talking.

"Lawrence wasn't hurt on the trip north." Meredith spoke directly to Harlowe. She set the photo in his lap and took his hand. "He was given up for adoption. A northern couple, children of your maternal grandmother's friend, took him in and raised him as their own. He became their son."

"They gave him away?" Harlowe couldn't have looked more stunned. Nor, for that matter, could Jem. "That makes no sense. No sense at all. My parents would never have given a child away." Distress carved deep wrinkles in his features. "Why would they do that? No, I don't believe it," he fumed. "You didn't know my parents, they loved us. They would never have done something like that. Not ever."

"And yet they did," Julia told him. She handed over copies of the ancestry information. "And for a very prudent reason at the time.

Your grandmother, Patrice's mother, was one-quarter African American."

Harlowe's eyes rounded.

"She passed for white up in New York, and when she fell in love with a Southern gentleman, he didn't care what her genetics were. They got married and had two children. They lost your uncle in a tragic accident, but Patrice grew up to be the toast of the town. We all know that. She fell in love with Sully Green, and they had a fairy-tale romance. A wonderful life. But something changed when your grandmother died, and our guess is that somehow Patrice discovered her heritage, and then she saw something in Lawrence—"

"That gorgeous head of hair and those luminous brown eyes," Julia added.

"We think that Lawrence's more exotic looks made Patrice nervous. We think they sent him north because your mother understood what could happen if people discovered she was passing for white. I can't say what else happened, but the genetics paint a whole new picture for us. Your parents didn't hurt Lawrence. Or anyone else. They saved him and you and your sisters from a reckoning they couldn't control."

Harlowe's face paled. His chin quivered. Two tears dripped from his pale brown eyes. He didn't seem to notice. "They gave him away."

"Harlowe—"

He raised his hand to quiet Meredith. She took the hint.

"You can't pretty it up," he said quietly. "You can't tie a bow around this and say it was for the best, because then you have to say 'whose best?' Not mine. Certainly not Lawrence's. And Wilma and Bertha, they never got a chance to know him. Love him. Play with him. He was a wonderful kid," he choked out on a half sob. "They could have moved. They could have moved to a place in the north and kept us together, couldn't they?" He stared at the two women, asking a question for which they had no answer. "So why did I find his baby book under Nanny's bed? Why was it messed up? Why was everything in life suddenly all messed up?" he demanded.

There was nothing Julia could say to make this better. She reached over and handed him a clutch of tissues as Meredith bowed her head in prayer.

But then Jem Baldwin reached for his bag. He slipped it open quietly and withdrew an antiquated book. A soot-smudged cloth-covered book that had *Our Baby* engraved in gold ink. And when he held it up, Harlowe's eyes widened. "His book." His face changed. His entire affect changed. "How did you find it? How did you get it? I never saw it again after the night I took the picture out of it," he exclaimed. "Tell me, man. How did you get Lawrence's book?"

Vermont
Fall 1937

There were no trains passing through until the next day, so Carolina took a seat in the small depot to wait. Her belly gurgled, not from hunger, but angst. Her insides churned with the unfairness of honesty. She clenched and unclenched

her hands, and when she finally dozed off, long after dark-
ness hid the tracks that marked the station, it was a broken
sleep, filled with images.

Exhausted, she boarded the train the next morning,
wishing she'd stayed silent. The truth had set her free, all
right. Free to begin again, leave a dear love and his children
behind, and find a new job.

You've done this before. You can do it again. Use your
head, not your heart, and forge on. You are an amazing
young woman. *Her mother's words of wisdom flooded her,*
and when she got off the train in New York's Mohawk Valley,
she wasted no time. Her small cache of funds would run out
if she didn't find a job quickly, so when she spotted a HELP
WANTED *sign in the hotel window, she hurried that way. A*
gruff-looking woman stood behind the counter. When she
spotted Carolina, she frowned. "We have no rooms available
at this time, miss. I'm sorry to say that, but the Hudson Hotel
might have something available."

"Is the job taken?" *Carolina lifted the handwritten plac-*
ard from the window. "I'm new in town and in need of work."

"As a hotel maid?" *Surprise lifted the woman's brows.*
"You have experience?"

"I've nannied for children, so cleaning up after them is
part of the job. This can't be much different, I suppose."

"Except you're dealing with men, most often, not children, and men can be a trial to a young, single woman. Our
housekeepers are not generally as comely as you are, and our
clientele changes daily."

She seemed genuinely concerned, but her words surprised Carolina. "So I can't have a job because I'm attractive?"

The woman flushed. "Sometimes it's better to avoid trouble than to court it. That's all I'm saying. And while jobs are scarce most places, we are seeing our share of WPA workers and projects and there are some rough men." The crease between her thick brows deepened. "Tough times make for tough people."

"I made cheese in Wisconsin, working with men. Working among them is not unknown to me."

"You made cheese?"

She nodded.

"Joseph Olmstead's got a busy shop over on Main West. They make the cheese in the back and sell it up front. He might be looking to hire someone, 'specially if you can fill both spots. You'd think in hard times folks would show up for work, but they don't always, and he's generally wearing three hats. Cheesemaker, salesman, and farmer, and he's not overly fond of the split. Tell him I sent you over."

"I will." She gripped the handle of her bag tightly. "And I thank you for the advice, Mrs.—"

"Drexler. Trudy Drexler, and welcome to Little Falls."

Carolina backed out the door, descended to the street level, and headed west until she spotted a sign for Olmstead Cheese. She walked in the front door, and when a balding fiftyish-something man came into the sales area, she stuck out her hand swiftly. "Trudy from the hotel sent me over, sir."

"*She did?*"

"*She said you might be looking to hire a helper who knows cheese. I spent four years at Dorcester Cheese in Wisconsin and brought the skills learned there back east. I'm comfortable setting cheese or working with customers. That would free you up to do the things you need to do, I expect.*"

"*You married?*"

"*I am not.*" *A clutch of sadness gripped her chest when she said that.*

Two customers walked in as a new train pulled out across the way. He lifted a brow their way, then addressed her. "*When can you start?*"

"*Now.*"

He breathed a sigh of relief and reached for her bag. "*I'll put this in the back.*"

She slipped off her traveling gloves and set her small satchel aside, then turned to the new customers. "*Ladies, how may I help you today?*"

Another customer came in, and then a small group of men, and by the late afternoon she'd sold dozens of pounds of Limburger, cheddar, and Swiss. When Joseph Olmstead came in to close up shop at six o'clock, he whistled lightly. "*You sold a week's worth of cheese in an afternoon?*"

"*Did I?*" *She lifted both hands.* "*It was busy, and the cheese kind of sells itself, doesn't it?*"

Joseph almost smiled. "*Let's say it seems to sell itself more when a smart salesperson is in the room.*"

"Thank you." Ah, to be considered smart and capable.

She loved that. She'd always loved that feeling, of being respected and well thought of. She'd had that in Vermont until she revealed her past. She'd had it in Savannah until she asked too many questions, and she'd had it in Wisconsin until she'd let her heart rule her head.

Now it would be the other way around.

She was done with her heart. She'd cage it soundly and live a quiet life. A life on her own, of her own, because when you let people in, their power to hurt you magnified, and she'd had enough of that to last a lifetime.

From this point forward no one else would get the chance.

Chapter Twenty-Six

JEM PASSED THE BOOK TO Harlowe. "Carolina Lambert was my great-grandmother."

Meredith faced him, shocked.

So did Julia.

Harlowe stared at Jem, then dropped his eyes to the book in front of him. He traced the gilt letters with one shaky finger. And then, with trembling hands, he opened the book.

Several folded pages slipped out. He caught one, but the others floated to the ground.

"Letters from my great-grandmother to her sister Virginia," Jem explained. "Virginia moved west in 1910. She was ten years older than Carolina, and they never saw one another again."

"But how did you get this?" Harlowe clutched the book in frail hands. "And you came here knowing more than we knew," he realized with a sudden flash of inspiration. "I hired this agency to find the truth about my brother so you wouldn't, but you knew it all along."

"I didn't." Jem shook his head firmly. "My grandfather was Lawson Engstrom, Carolina's only child. My mother is Lawson's daughter, Lorah Engstrom Baldwin. Carolina moved to Wisconsin when she was fired from her job with the Greens. She worked in a cheese house, then married my great-grandfather a few years later, but his mother didn't approve of her or the marriage, and she was a hard-hearted woman. Carolina went east when Lawson, my grandfather, was just five years old. She just up and left, and when my grandfather grew up, he wanted to find his mother.

"He remembered his mother being kind and good," he continued. "Quite different from the harsh grandmother who raised him. His father remarried and had three more children with Gretchen, his second wife, and they never said much about Lawson's real mother, but every now and again he'd hear them whisper and it bothered him. Why would a mother leave a child? Especially a child she loved?"

He paused, staring at the book. Then he continued his part of the story. "Grandpa was young when he set out to discover the truth. He searched out every nook and cranny to trace his mother's footsteps."

"You get that from him," Julia noted.

He accepted that with a nod. "He hounded his father for every bit of information he could. Eventually he pieced enough together to trace Carolina to Vermont, then New York. And that's where Carolina stayed, all alone until she died of tuberculosis."

He scrunched his face then, as if puzzled and frustrated. "When I became a writer, Grandpa brought me everything he'd found. The book, the notes his aunt Virginia had saved, and his interviews with people in Vermont and in New York. When I read them, I saw this horrible cause-and-effect, perpetuated by the Greens. That's what I supposed, anyway," he told them. "Everything pointed to them doing something heinous, and when they tried to cover it up, Carolina's life became collateral damage. She couldn't stand the guilt, you see." He leaned forward and pressed his hands together. "Not knowing what happened hounded her all of her days. She'd lost a child she loved, had to leave others she loved, and lost her best friend, all at once. And then forced out with no money, no credentials, and very little trust in anything or anyone. I will admit that the emptiness of her life grabbed hold of me," he told them softly. "I came here wanting to find the truth. Wanting to make the Green family pay, wanting to expose them for what they were, but this—"

He indicated Meredith and Julia with a wave of his hand.

"This changes everything. The Greens weren't the monsters I wanted them to be. They were victims of the times, like so many others. But what an awful way to live and a wretched choice to make."

Harlowe didn't seem to notice the tears trickling down his cheeks. "Is Lawrence gone now?" he whispered but then blinked twice. "Of course he is," he scolded himself. Then he looked at Meredith and Julia. "Did he have a good life at least? I pray he did."

Now Julia slipped him a different piece of paper. It was a print of a mid-twentieth-century movie flyer featuring an all-star cast. "Recognize anyone, Harlowe?" she asked softly.

He looked at the flyer then drew his eyes up to the other three, appearing shocked once again. But this time in a good way. "Larry Leigh is really Lawrence Green?"

Meredith nodded. "As you know, he went on to have an amazing career on stage and in some of the biggest blockbuster movies of that time."

"He was a family favorite," he breathed. "My parents used to fund the shows that brought Broadway musicals to Savannah, and he was in several of them." He met Meredith's and Julia's gazes and sighed. "They knew. They brought him to them because they couldn't go to him," he whispered.

"So they did the best they could." Jem took a deep breath. Then he turned to Meredith and Julia. "I'm sorry I suspected you two of sabotage. The police department contacted me that they've found my computer in a suburb outside of Charleston, and that they need to keep it as evidence."

"Although if none of us presses charges against a man who worked hard to save a legacy—" Meredith said.

"And kind of freaked when things began spinning out of control," Julia added.

"Maybe we can avoid having one more victim," Meredith finished. "Something to think about," she added, and then she reached over and gave Harlowe a gentle hug. "We've tired you, my friend. But in a good way, I hope."

In one hand Harlowe clutched his brother's baby book. The other hand gripped the flyer. "It is a good way," he whispered. He held tight to both when he looked up. "The very best way. Thank you." His gaze included Meredith and Julia, then shifted to Jem. "And I wish good writing to you, sir."

Jem swiped a hand through his hair when he stood. "I have no doubt it will be the best book I've ever done. And Mr. Green?" he added in a deferential tone. "It will be dedicated to you. To the boy who never forgot his little brother, the sweet petal that fell by the wayside."

Harlowe sighed. "If you'd known him, you'd understand why," he said softly, but then he raised the glossy flyer a little higher. "His story might have been changed, but his legacy lived on. And that's a mighty good ending right there."

Meredith touched Julia's arm as Myla showed them to the big front door. "I couldn't agree more."

Little Falls, New York
1948

"Miss Lambert is here!" Joseph's great-granddaughter charged into the cheese shop like she always did, as if there was so much life to be lived. She'd become Carolina's fun companion over the past decade. Following her around, asking questions, nosing into business, ever curious. "We didn't expect you today. Grandpa said you were taking a day off, and I was wretchedly disappointed."

"Oh, you dear thing." Carolina stood up to greet the girl and her attractive mother. "You make my heart sing, BeeBee. And I had to come in today because—" She coughed then, and for a moment, the cough wouldn't be suppressed. Then all was fine. "Mr. Gilder took ill, and I didn't want your grandfather to be shorthanded in the spring setting season. It's a busy time for farmers and cheesemakers."

"I asked my grandpa if we could go fishing, and he said, 'Girl'"—BeeBee put her hands on her hips in imitation—"'it's spring and this is a dairy farm. What are you thinking, child?'"

"That's the way of it." Carolina patted BeeBee's shoulder. "To everything there is a season, sweet BeeBee, and we do ourselves a good turn when we recognize that for what it is."

"Like this is wedding season in the north," her mother added. "Folks line up to schedule May and June weddings, before the bugs and humidity make it uncomfortable for everyone."

"Did you ever get married, Miss Lambert? Like ever?"

It was the surprise of the question that caught Carolina off guard, and she nodded before she could help herself, then regretted the motion when BeeBee delved further.

"Did he die? Did you have kids?"

For over ten years she'd lived a quiet life in this small town nestled not far from the railroad tracks that brought her here. She'd lived alone. She was friendly but didn't covet friends. The only thing she'd embraced fully was her job and her faith, and it had been enough. Enough to keep her anchored and unhurt, but BeeBee's quick question speared that old rod through her heart like a brand-new wound.

"BeeBee, we mustn't ask personal questions. It isn't done," her mother spoke sharply, then addressed Carolina in a quieter tone. "I'm sorry, Miss Carolina, I don't know what's gotten into her. At ten years old, she knows better."

"But did you?" BeeBee pressed, and was it the earnest tone or the beseeching look that made Carolina nod again? She wasn't sure, but nod she did.

"I did, once. A little boy, half your age. His name was Lawson," she explained, and stooped down slightly because if she went too low, it wasn't all that easy to get back up as the years marched on. "He was beautiful, like you. Outspoken too. And I loved him very much."

"Where is he?" BeeBee breathed.

"I don't know. We lost touch a long time ago, and I don't know where he is or what he's doing. But I pray for him, every day. Like I do for you," she added simply. "Because when a child captures your heart, they manage to claim a part of your soul too."

"Thank you for praying for me!" BeeBee clutched her hand, and when Carolina winced, she loosened her grip. "Oh, sorry, Miss Carolina! I didn't mean to squeeze so tight, I'm just so excited to see you again. Can we do cheese this week? I'm all caught up on learning and school won't be out for weeks and weeks, but you're the best cheesemaker around, and even MawMaw says so."

"When your mother says it's all right, we'll make cheese. I've been sharpening up some new skills as French cheeses become more popular, and I could use a helper, for certain."

"I think our smart girl can come over after school this week," said her mother. "BeeBee, homework first, as always, but then you can come and help Miss Carolina in the cheese rooms."

"It will be my best week ever," the girl declared and when she squeezed Carolina's hand this time, it was with the gentle touch of respect—and love. And Carolina had to look away to hide the quick rush of tears to her eyes.

She'd meant what she said. She prayed for her blessed boy every single day, and too, for his forgiveness. Someday—

Maybe—

That would happen.

Chapter Twenty-Seven

"Unbelievable, isn't it?" Julia raised her glass of Diet Dr Pepper to toast the end of their second successful case. "We did it. I kind of thought this one would be impossible, but it wasn't, so I stand corrected."

"Great teamwork," Meredith noted with a smile that included Julia, Maggie Lu, and Carmen. Carmen had graciously driven Maggie Lu over to Julia's house.

"And the late-night lasagna was nothing to be taken lightly," Julia told her mother as B.J. brought a pitcher of tea to them on Julia's beautiful wraparound porch. They'd all gathered to celebrate a job well done and to welcome Beau home. "Thanks for jumping in on that, Mom."

"My pleasure." B.J. smiled.

"I'm glad that Martin Linkletter is getting nothing more than a warning," Julia noted. "After we met with him, I wanted to recommend leniency, but then I realized that as a retired judge, it's out of my hands, so I was even happier when the Savannah court agreed."

"After we all dropped charges," said Meredith. "But I'm glad we agreed to do that, because I didn't want any more sad stories to come of all this. Let the time of peace and love reign. This way he can go on teaching about history and tolerance, and the documentary lives on."

"Amen to that," noted Carmen. She put a peach pie onto the table, and B.J. followed with fresh whipped cream.

The humidity had broken after the tropical storm a few days before. A breeze sifted through the trees, and the temperature had dropped to the upper seventies, a rare respite in June.

"And we got an email from Arnold today, stating that our offices should be ready for occupancy by the end of June, so that's a blessing," Meredith went on. "Although I'll miss our regular supply of baked goods," she told Carmen, laughing.

"I'll work remotely on occasion," Carmen promised. "From your kitchen."

"Deal," Meredith declared. "And if either of my sons shows up, try not to hurt him too badly. Okay?"

Carmen blushed, but everyone else just laughed.

Julia looped her arm around Meredith's shoulders before her friend sat down. "I had a few doubts this time around," she told Meredith, and didn't care that everyone else was listening. "Not in you. You were marvelous. You taught me a lot, and I went into this investigating venture thinking it would be a breeze. That all I needed to do was see the common sense of the situation, but you and Maggie Lu taught me that I need to go beyond that, to the human essence of the situation. And honestly, ladies"—she breathed deeply and sighed—"that has made all the difference. Thank you. Thank you both." She included Maggie Lu in those words. "Because from now on, I'll look beyond the obvious and into the heart of the matter. Every time."

"Hear, hear." Meredith raised her glass of tea.

So did Maggie Lu. And when the three women clinked glasses, the pinging sound of success made all three smile.

Dear Reader,

I loved writing this beautiful story of how the past creeps up on the present, even when we least expect it. And what fun to work with these two heroines, Julia and Meredith! With the old-world wisdom of Maggie Lu and the frankness of Carmen, these ladies are unique, but none of them is the type to give up the fight. Building a new business isn't the kind of thing one does casually at any age, and that gives me more reason to love them!

Savannah's beautiful setting provides an ideal backdrop for our "steel magnolias" as they tackle old secrets and new challenges. While we tiptoe into past wrongs, we charge full steam into new adventures that delve into all walks of life.

I hope you love this meld of past and present. This Yankee loves dabbling in the South, raising a glass of sweet tea or Cheerwine, and making Southern comfort food for my northern family. All in the name of research, of course!

Sending blessings!
—Ruthy

About the Author

MULTIPUBLISHED *USA TODAY* BESTSELLING AUTHOR Ruth Logan Herne has over fifty published novels and novellas, a big family, a pumpkin farm, and way too many animals (although you can never have too many dogs, right?). She loves taking part in these Guideposts collections, and she loves hearing from readers! When she's not writing, she's definitely not cleaning, but she might be growing thousands of chrysanthemums or pumpkin plants, tending tomatoes, cleaning water gardens, or playing with babies or puppies. Although she does do windows because she's got a thing about clean windows—and that can never be considered a bad thing! You can find her on the web at ruthloganherne.com, yankeebellecafe. blogspot.com, friend her on Facebook, or email her directly at loganherne@gmail.com.

An Armchair Tour of Savannah

I AM A HUGE FAN of ice cream. I have a favorite frozen custard place here in Western New York where the gals all know me by name, so when I discovered Leopold's Ice Cream in Savannah—and saw their five thousand-plus reviews—I had to do a piece on it.

There's something so hometown-good about an ice cream shop or sandwich shop that stands the test of time. Don't we all remember a favorite stopping spot from our childhood or dating years? Up here it would likely be a Greek diner or candymaker and ice cream shop, and that's true in Savannah too. Leopold's Ice Cream owes its heritage to a family of Greek immigrants and a beneficent uncle who showed three boys the ropes of the business.

Their web page embraces the history of these three:

"Leopold's Ice Cream was founded in 1919 by three brothers from Greece. They learned the art of candy and dessert making from an uncle who had already settled in America. George, Peter, and Basil Leopold perfected their secret formulas and created the now world-famous Leopold's Ice Cream."

Open daily from 11:00 to 11:00, this famous eatery draws locals and tourists. I was happy to feature their ice cream as part of our

fictional Downhome Diner menu, because we small business owners stick together. Their long list of delicious frozen confections are
balanced with an old-time soup-and-sandwich type menu, which
is perfect, because at Leopold's, one should always save room for
dessert!

PEACHES-N-CREAM PIE

(A favorite at the Downhome Diner! With a scoop of that famous
Leopold's Vanilla Bean ice cream, of course.)

Ingredients:

2 piecrust pastries (homemade
or store-bought)

1½ cup sugar

⅓ cup flour

1½ tablespoons quick
tapioca

Dash salt

1½ cup heavy cream, divided

½ teaspoon vanilla

6 cups sliced peaches, fresh or
frozen (thawed and drained
and patted dry)

Directions:

Combine sugar, flour, tapioca, and salt in large bowl. Set aside 3
tablespoons of cream. Combine remaining cream with vanilla. Add
to sugar mixture. Add peaches. Mix gently to coat peaches. Allow to
sit for 15 to 20 minutes.

Put bottom pastry in 9-inch deep-dish pie pan. Trim edge to
about 1 inch past pie plate edge.

Pour peach mixture into bottom crust.

Roll out top crust. Place crust over pie, crimp edges, and cut four slits in the top, evenly spaced on four sides to vent.

Once crust is on, brush with remaining cream and sprinkle with sugar.

Bake at 400 degrees for 45 to 55 minutes, until golden brown and bubbly. I cover the edge crust with thin strips of foil to keep it from getting overdone. Cool and then store leftovers in fridge.

Read on for a sneak peek of another exciting book
in the Savannah Secrets series!

Double Trouble

BY GABRIELLE MEYER

SUNSHINE GLIMMERED THROUGH THE LEAVES of the live oaks and magnolia trees as Meredith Bellefontaine sat beside her son, Chase, who drove her SUV through the historic streets of Savannah. Since losing her husband, Ron, almost two years ago, she had come to cherish these rare moments with her grown son even more and tried not to take them for granted.

Outside, the July sun baked the brick sidewalks of East Charlton Street, where Meredith had lived since she had inherited the three-story row house from her great-granddaddy. Inside the vehicle, the air-conditioning felt pleasant, but more importantly, the cool climate would help protect the integrity of the priceless heirlooms riding in the back seat and on her lap.

"Careful," she said to Chase for the fifth time since leaving the Savannah National Bank. "Maybe we should have buckled the writing desk in before we left."

Chase only smiled at Meredith's fretting and carefully turned right onto Habersham Street. Her house sat on the corner of East

Charlton and Habersham, and boasted access to Troup Square, one of the smaller and lesser known of the twenty-four squares laid out by the founders of Savannah. An afternoon bridal shower was in full swing, if Meredith guessed correctly. White tables and chairs, beautiful floral arrangements, and a whole host of women in large hats eagerly watched a young lady open a pile of gifts. Behind the bride-to-be was the Victorian armillary mounted on six bronze turtles. The large structure looked like several circles intertwining in a globe, representing the celestial relationships.

In one corner of the square, opposite Meredith's stucco Italianate home, was the quaint brown Unitarian Universalist Church, which was rumored to be the location where organist James Piermont wrote the beloved Christmas song "Jingle Bells." And in the center was the popular cast-iron pet water fountain. Troup Square wasn't the grandest or the most beautiful of the squares, but it was Meredith's favorite, and its gravel paths, lush green grass, and cozy benches always made her smile.

"The writing desk will be fine," Chase reassured her as he took one more right turn onto Macon Street and parked the car in Meredith's spot directly behind her house. His voice grew deep in mock seriousness. "As long as I can get it into the house without dropping it."

"Don't tease." Meredith put her hand on his arm, her pulse picking up speed, even though she knew he was joking. "Two hundred and eighty-six years of family history are represented in that desk."

"Not to mention centuries of mystery that will finally be revealed." As a history professor at Emory University in Atlanta, Chase was just as excited to examine the family heirloom as Meredith. It had been in the bank safe since the late 1950s when Ron's aunt, Temperance

Bellefontaine, had inherited it and then hidden it away again. She had refused to take it out, no matter how many times Meredith and Chase had asked. Now, after her death, she had left it to Meredith in her will. Even though Meredith was only a Bellefontaine by marriage, Aunt Temperance had wanted it to go to her because Meredith had been the president of the Savannah Historical Society and would eventually pass it on to one of her sons, keeping it in the Bellefontaine family.

"I wish I could stay for the weekend to look over the desk and the diary," Chase said as he put the car in PARK. "But hopefully I can get back here in the next few weeks." He had made the three-and-a-half-hour trip from his home in Atlanta to accompany her to the bank but had to leave within the hour to return for an important meeting.

The diary he spoke of lay in Meredith's lap. With white cotton gloves, she had removed it from the writing desk at the bank and slipped it into an acid-free envelope. "I've been longing to get my hands on this diary for years," she said. "Maybe now we can have it properly preserved."

"And finally learn about Anna Coles and her connection to the pirate Blackbeard." Chase wiggled his eyebrows in anticipation. He loved history, but he also loved historical lore, especially pirate legends. "I heard the buzz about the diary all the way in Atlanta. A lot of people will be excited to find out what the diary has to tell us."

"I'm not as concerned about the pirate connection, since I doubt there is any," Meredith said. "I'm more excited to learn about the early days of Savannah." She opened her door and gingerly held the diary as she stepped out of the SUV. "So little is known about the original colonists, it's a shame Aunt Temperance kept the diary hidden in a safe these past sixty years."

"And her mother before her." Chase also exited the car and opened the back door. Meredith came around the vehicle to watch as he gently removed the small writing desk from the back seat. Closed, it looked like a simple rectangular box made of walnut. Brass handles on either end, as well as a brass lock in the center, were the only adornments. Over the years, it had been scratched and dented, but it was in surprisingly good shape. It opened in two halves at the hinges and presented a sloped, hard surface to write on. Under the writing surface was a compartment for paper and books. The other side had wooden squares meant to hold ink bottles and pens. "I wonder why each generation of Bellefontaines chose to keep it hidden."

Meredith shrugged and cringed when the desk bumped into the side of the car as Chase pulled it out. "Maybe they just didn't care."

"That can't be true."

"Then why didn't Aunt Temperance talk about the diary or let us read it?" The older woman had refused to discuss the diary—and almost appeared scared of it. Meredith had never understood her reticence.

When the desk was clear of the vehicle, Meredith closed the door and walked ahead of Chase to the brown wooden gate at the back of the row house. After slipping the key into the lock, she pushed the gate open into a small courtyard with a wall fountain. The delicate sound of trickling water and birds tweeting in a nearby magnolia greeted them.

"Maybe we'll finally find out why they kept it hidden." Chase waited for Meredith to go ahead of him and open the back door into the house.

"I've already been contacted by five different newspapers in Georgia, Florida, and South Carolina." Meredith unlocked her house door and opened it for Chase to walk into the back hall. "There's so much speculation about the diary and its contents. When news leaked that Aunt Temperance had died and I was the heir to the diary, I spent hours staving off curious people."

"What have you said?" Chase asked.

"I've declined to answer until I know more about the diary." The back entry wasn't very large, with its tile floor and ornate hooks on the wall. Four steps led down to the raised basement and seven steps led up to the main floor of the house. "But it hasn't stopped them from reporting on the little that is known about the diary. Most of it is hearsay and rumors."

"Some of my colleagues have read the articles online. Everyone thinks we'll finally find Blackbeard's long-lost treasure. It's believed to be the largest pirate treasure still hidden today." Chase's blue eyes, so like his father's, twinkled from the prospect.

"Don't tell me you're getting gold fever." Meredith tried hard not to chastise her adult sons, but sometimes the mother in her couldn't be controlled.

"Wouldn't it be fun to find it, if for no other reason than the historical value?"

"This diary and writing desk are the only treasures I need." Meredith closed the back door and indicated the steps leading to the lower level. "I want to keep the desk in the study."

Chase maneuvered toward the stairs, and Meredith found herself holding her breath again. "Be careful."

Thankfully, Chase was patient with her apprehension and took his time going down the stairs.

The house had been updated just before Ron passed away. Meredith had kept the character and integrity of the 1870s home intact but had updated the colors and the flow of the layout. At the bottom of the steps, they entered a large family room with a low, beamed ceiling, dark wood floors, and comfortable furniture. A redbrick fireplace, white built-in cabinets, and plush rugs gave the room a homey feel. At the far end, facing East Charlton Street and the front of the house, a bright study beckoned. Large windows let in the south-facing sunshine.

"Are you sure you want this in the study?" Chase asked as he entered the cozy room.

"I think it's best." Meredith moved some papers on her desk aside and made a spot for the writing desk. "The safe is in here."

Behind the gold-gilded picture frame of *Washington Crossing the Delaware*, a hidden safe was tucked into the wall. It wasn't large, but it held Meredith's most important documents and would be the perfect place to store the diary.

A shadow passed just outside the bay window facing East Charlton Street. It wasn't uncommon for pedestrians to walk in front of Meredith's home, especially so close to Troup Square—but this person caught Meredith's eye. Something about the way he walked and carried himself brought a twinge of grief to her heart and forced her to look closer. The man was tall, his shoulders broad and solid. Everything about him, from his salt-and-pepper hair to his strong jawline, looked strikingly similar to Ron.

With a racing heart and sweating palms, Meredith moved closer to the window.

The man had stopped at the base of the curved stairway that led from the street to the front door. From where she stood, she could only see the side of his face as he looked up at the house.

"Mom?" Chase sounded concerned. "What's wrong?"

Meredith couldn't find her voice. It stuck in her throat like a lump, choking her and cutting off her air.

The man turned and met Meredith's startled gaze. His eyes, the exact shade of Ron's and Chase's, grew wide.

Without stopping to explain, Meredith rushed out of the study, up the stairs, and into the main floor entry.

"Mom?" Chase was close behind her. "Where are you going?"

Meredith fumbled with the locks on the front door and finally yanked it open. She stumbled onto the stoop, but the man was no longer there. She looked toward Troup Square, and then down East Charlton Street, but he was not there either.

"You're scaring me," Chase said when he stepped onto the stoop and put his hand on Meredith's shoulder. "What's going on?"

Meredith started to move down the steps, but Chase held her back, forcing her to turn and face him.

"What is it, Mom?"

Swallowing around the lump, Meredith stopped and took a deep breath. "Your father."

"What?" Chase shook his head, a frown marring his handsome face.

"I—I just saw him, at the foot of these steps." She pointed at the spot where the man had been standing. "But he left."

"You saw Dad?" Concern filled Chase's eyes. "Mom, you're not making any sense."

"It looked just like him." She continued to scan the street, desperate to see the man again.

"Mom." Chase repositioned himself to stand between her and the street so she was forced to look at him. "You know it wasn't Dad. He's gone."

"I know he's gone, Chase." Her heart was still pounding hard, but the initial shock began to wear off. "I'm not given to flights of fancy—but I'm not blind either. The man looked exactly like your father."

"There are probably a lot of men who look like Dad."

"This man could have been his twin."

"Maybe Dad had a twin he never told you about." Chase's soft voice teased and was likely meant to make her smile, but she couldn't bring herself to oblige him. He was her peacemaker, always trying to ease a tense moment with his sense of humor. He turned her toward the house and gently nudged her back inside. "Don't let it bother you, Mom."

How could it not bother her? She'd just seen a man who looked exactly like her dead husband standing outside her house.

It was the most bothersome thing she'd ever encountered.

A Note from the Editors

We hope you enjoy the Savannah Secrets series, created by the Books and Inspirational Media Division of Guideposts, a nonprofit organization that touches millions of lives every day through products and services that inspire, encourage, help you grow in your faith, and celebrate God's love in every aspect of your daily life.

Thank you for making a difference with your purchase of this book, which helps fund our many outreach programs to military personnel, prisons, hospitals, nursing homes, and educational institutions. To learn more, visit GuidepostsFoundation.org.

We also maintain many useful and uplifting online resources. Visit Guideposts.org to read true stories of hope and inspiration, access OurPrayer network, sign up for free newsletters, download free e-books, join our Facebook community, and follow our stimulating blogs.

To learn about other Guideposts publications, including the best-selling devotional *Daily Guideposts*, go to ShopGuideposts.org, call (800) 932-2145, or write to Guideposts, PO Box 5815, Harlan, Iowa 51593.

Sign up for the
Guideposts Fiction Newsletter
and stay up-to-date on the books you love!

You'll get sneak peeks of new releases, recommendations from other Guideposts readers, and special offers just for you . . .
and it's FREE!

Just go to Guideposts.org/Newsletters
today to sign up.

Find more inspiring stories in these best-loved Guideposts fiction series!

Mysteries of Lancaster County

Follow the Classen sisters as they unravel clues and uncover hidden secrets in Mysteries of Lancaster County. As you get to know these women and their friends, you'll see how God brings each of them together for a fresh start in life.

Secrets of Wayfarers Inn

Retired schoolteachers find themselves owners of an old warehouse-turned-inn that is filled with hidden passages, buried secrets, and stunning surprises that will set them on a course to puzzling mysteries from the Underground Railroad.

Tearoom Mysteries Series

Mix one stately Victorian home, a charming lakeside town in Maine, and two adventurous cousins with a passion for tea and hospitality. Add a large scoop of intriguing mystery, and sprinkle generously with faith, family, and friends, and you have the recipe for *Tearoom Mysteries*.

Ordinary Women of the Bible

Richly imagined stories—based on facts from the Bible—have all the plot twists and suspense of a great mystery, while bringing you fascinating insights on what it was like to be a woman living in the ancient world.

To learn more about these books, visit Guideposts.org/Shop